THE ATLAS OF FOOD

EDITED BY Genny Gallo

ILLUSTRATION BY Annalisa Beghelli

WSkids
WHITE STAR KIDS

How many different ways are there
to discover the world?

You do not necessarily have to get on a cruise ship or a jumbo jet.
Have a seat on the sofa, by yourself or with your mom and dad
if you like, and start turning the pages of this book. You will soon
discover **what they eat in the Amazon rainforest**
or how **chicken is cooked in India** or even which **insects**
native Australians prefer for a snack.

Close your eyes and it will not be long before you start
smelling the aromas and hearing the fire crackling under
the grill pan. You will see the golden color of delicious,
chocolate dipped churros and feel the softness
of a warm loaf of **challah bread.**

Explore the **maps**, choose the **names of the dishes** that
intrigue you the most and read about them in their descriptions.
Then **have fun locating them on the map** so you can
see in which region of the country they are typical. Let your
fingers walk you through each nation. You will find new dishes
and new flavors and the discovery game can start all over again!

HAVE A GOOD AND DELECTABLE READ!

CONTENTS

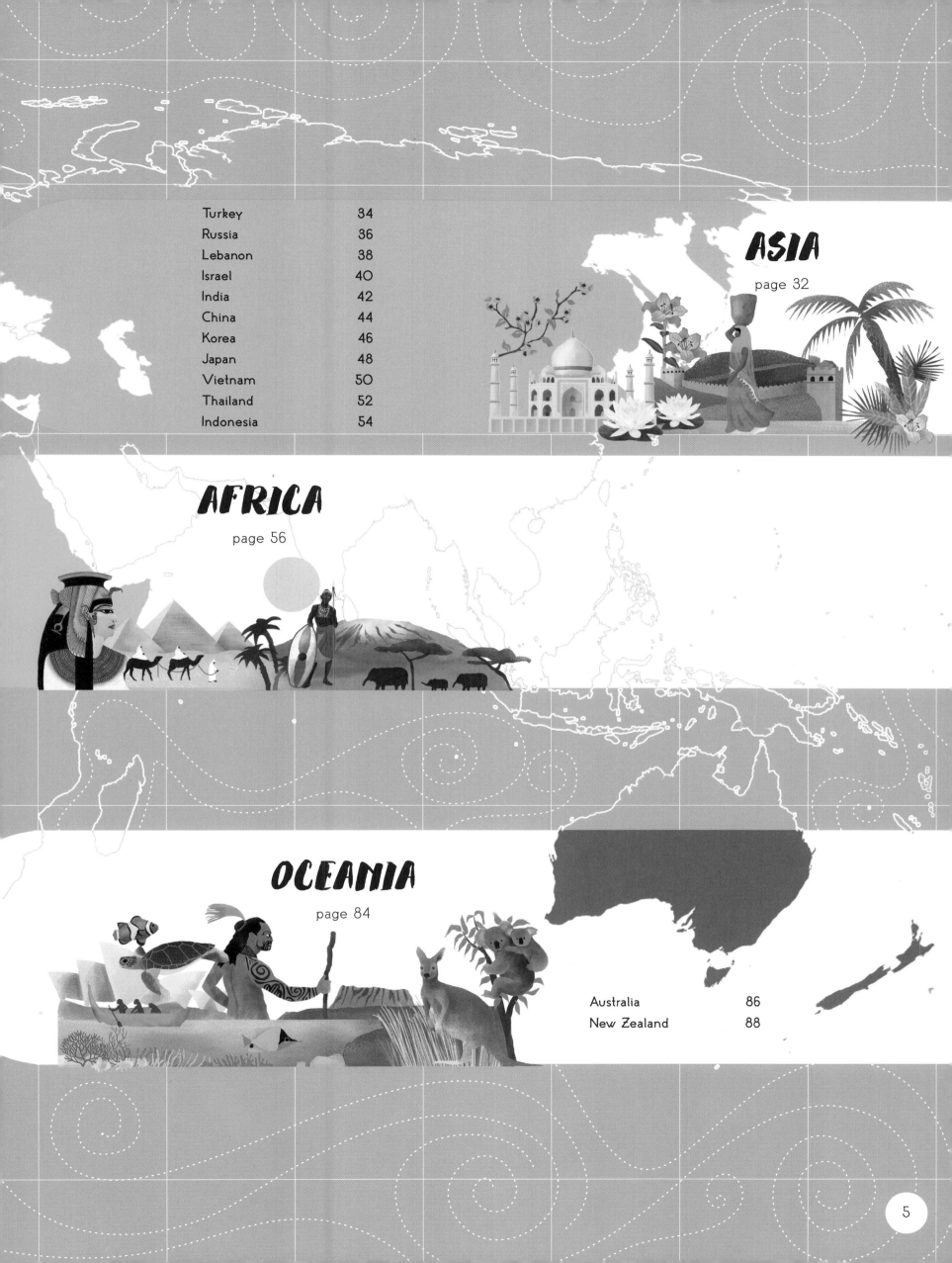

ASIA

page 32

AFRICA

page 56

OCEANIA

page 84

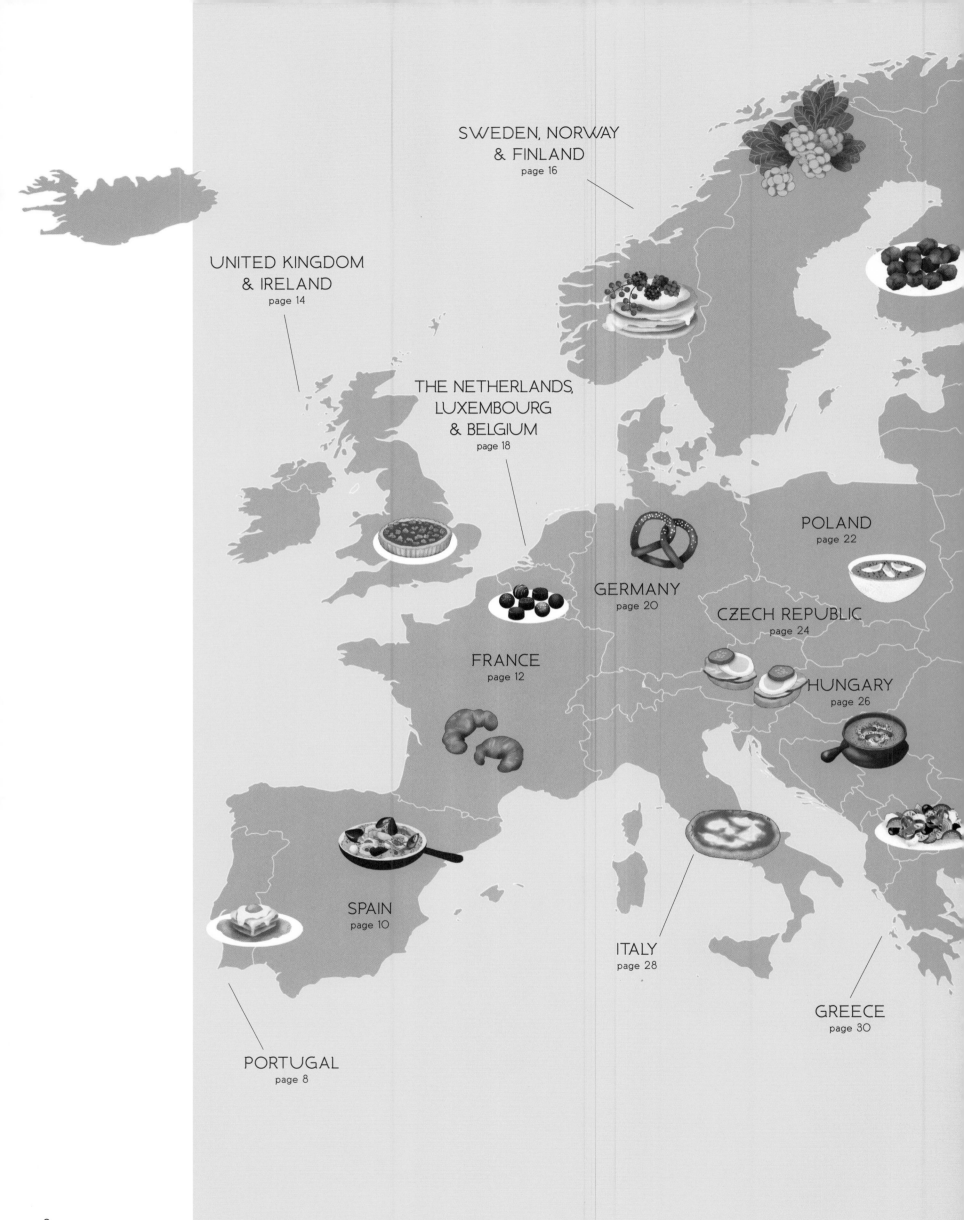

EUROPE

IN THESE COUNTRIES THE SECRETS AND FLAVORS OF THE WORLD'S MOST FAMOUS DISHES HAVE BEEN PASSED DOWN THROUGH THE CENTURIES.

For a long time, Europe was the cultural center of the world and it exported its cuisine and its dishes to nearly every country around the globe: pizza, croissants, brie cheese and pasta with marinara sauce can be found almost anywhere you go. UNESCO has recognized many European cuisines as Intangible Cultural Heritage of Humanity.

The feather in Europe's cap is undoubtedly the Mediterranean diet common to all the countries on the Mediterranean Sea. Not much more than vegetables, grains, pasta and fish make up this style of cooking and eating—universally recognized as the healthiest, a sort of fountain of youth.

But Europe is much more than the countries on the Mediterranean. The northern and central regions consume vast amounts of meat and cheese and, in fact, have created some of the best cheeses in the world.

1
SARDINHAS ASSADAS

Grilled sardines, a typical dish in Lisbon, can be found in food stands along the street as well as in restaurants. They are usually served with lemon and boiled potatoes.

2
BOLO DO CACO

In Madeira you can taste this flat bread flavored with garlic and parsley. It is heated on a fiery hot sheet of basalt to make it crisp on the outside and soft on the inside.

3
ARROZ DE PATO

A rice dish with stewed duck is covered with slices of chorizo and baked in the oven to give it a crunchy crust. It is typical in Portugal's hinterland.

4
PASTÉIS DE BELÉM

The Catholic nuns of the Mosteiro do Jerónimos in Lisbon created this sweet puff pastry filled with cream and covered with sugar and cinnamon. Today, the best ones are sold in the Belém district of Lisbon.

5
TORTA DE AZEITÃO

This soft, spongy cake is covered in sugar and egg yolk then rolled into its traditional tubular shape.

PORTUGAL

More than 500 miles of coastline and 300 days of sun every year: Portugal is a paradise of sun, beaches and inexpensive living. Deeply rooted traditions, an ample variety of readily available raw materials from both the land and the sea, and the mixture of cultures that have passed through this land characterize Portugal's cuisine. The country's fishermen catch crustaceans, shrimp, calamari, cuttlefish, octopus, clams and lobsters in the Atlantic Ocean every day while the dry land puts beef, poultry and pork on the table.

As soon as you sit down, you'll be served hot bread with olives and other snacks like cheese or fish dip. This enjoyable little appetizer called "coperto" meaning cover is an integral part of local hospitality.

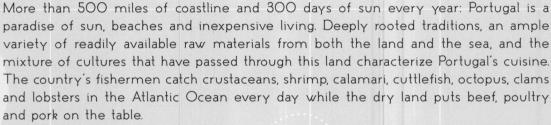

The Azores

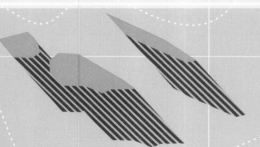

SALT COD FRITTERS

Finely chop 200 g (7 oz) of soaked, boiled salt codfish and mix it with 300 g (11 oz) of boiled potatoes, 2 eggs, a pinch of salt and some parsley. Knead the mixture till it is soft, then roll it into little balls. Fry the balls in boiling oil and enjoy them while they are hot.

8

COZIDO À PORTUGUESA

Mixed meats, vegetables and beans are the base of this stew. The broth from the stew is also used to cook rice.

9

AÇORDA

This bread soup is prepared with stale white bread, shrimp, tomatoes, eggs and garlic. In the Alentejo region's traditional version, *sopa a la alenteja*, the eggs are omitted and the shrimp are substituted with clams.

10

ALHEIRA AND CHORIZO

Both are typical cured meats of the area. The first is a chicken sausage with bread, garlic, lard and a yellowish–red spice called annatto. The second one resembles the types of hot salami frequently found in southern Europe.

11

PORCO À ALENTEJANA

This nourishing dish is an intriguing mix of pork and clams cooked in a cataplana, a clam–shaped pan traditionally made of copper.

12

PÃO CASEIRO

This homemade bread, typical of the internal regions, is made with whatever kind of flour is available. It is a common accompaniment to traditional soups and stews.

13

CABRITO ASSADO

You can find this specialty all over the country— roasted kid goat with generous side dishes of rice, roasted potatoes and vegetables.

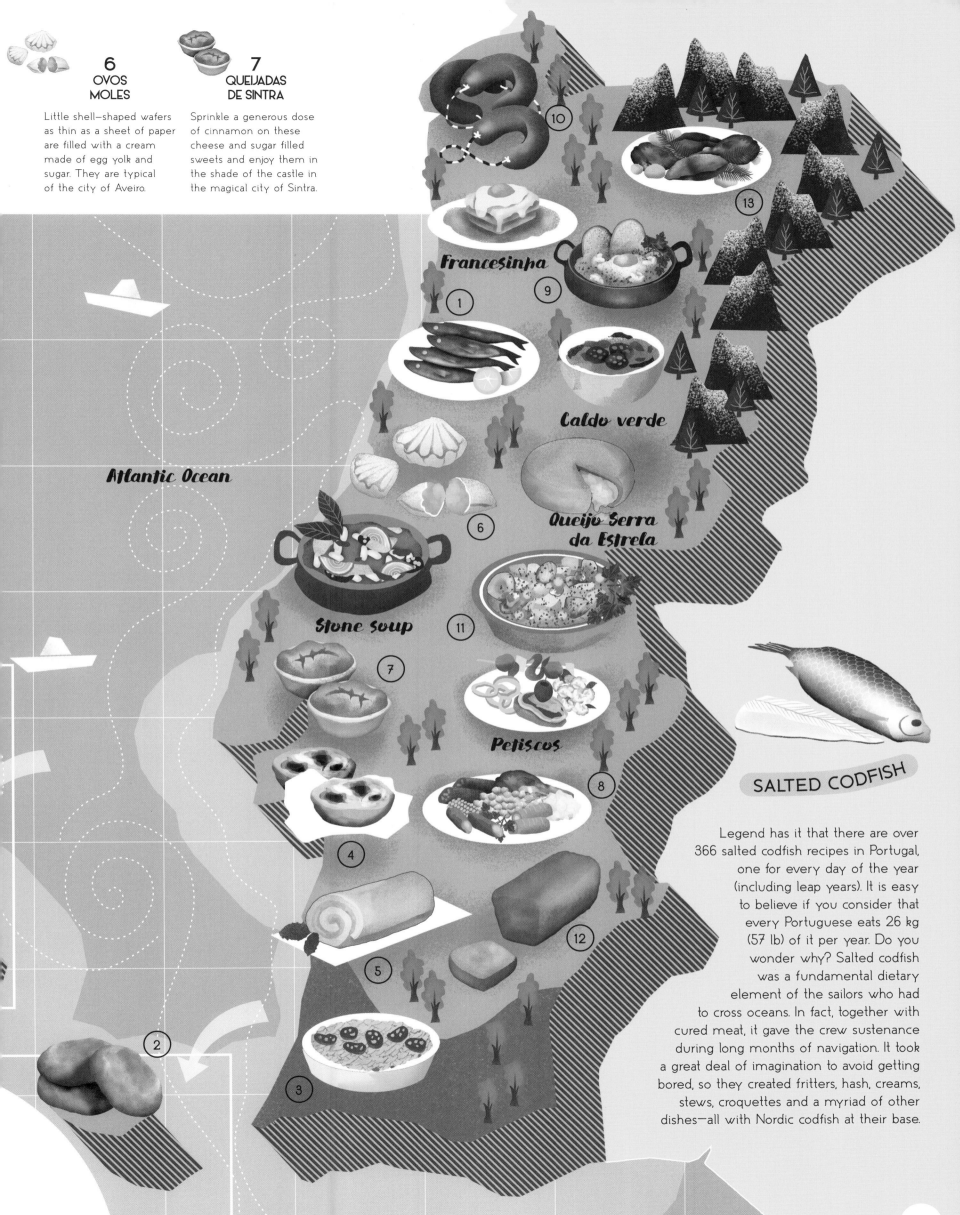

6 OVOS MOLES

Little shell–shaped wafers as thin as a sheet of paper are filled with a cream made of egg yolk and sugar. They are typical of the city of Aveiro.

7 QUEIJADAS DE SINTRA

Sprinkle a generous dose of cinnamon on these cheese and sugar filled sweets and enjoy them in the shade of the castle in the magical city of Sintra.

Atlantic Ocean

Francesinha

Caldo verde

Queijo Serra da Estrela

Stone soup

Petiscos

SALTED CODFISH

Legend has it that there are over 366 salted codfish recipes in Portugal, one for every day of the year (including leap years). It is easy to believe if you consider that every Portuguese eats 26 kg (57 lb) of it per year. Do you wonder why? Salted codfish was a fundamental dietary element of the sailors who had to cross oceans. In fact, together with cured meat, it gave the crew sustenance during long months of navigation. It took a great deal of imagination to avoid getting bored, so they created fritters, hash, creams, stews, croquettes and a myriad of other dishes—all with Nordic codfish at their base.

1
TAPAS

You cannot spend the evening in a Spanish bar or pub without tasting tapas. These bites of assorted dishes originated in Andalusia, where little portions of food were served to "plug" the glasses of sherry that were downed during long nights of drinking.

2
ANDALUSIAN GAZPACHO

Peppers, tomatoes, cucumbers and bread are the basis for this cold soup that was originally intended as a cooling snack for the hired hands on scorching summer days.

3
PULPO A LA GALLEGA

This is a simple dish of octopus and potatoes, frequently prepared on holidays. Octopus is a common ingredient in coastal cuisine.

4
COCIDO MADRILEÑO

This nourishing stew made with chickpeas, meats and vegetables is cooked over a slow fire. It is generally served in stages; first the broth with thin noodles, then the chickpeas with the vegetables and finally the pork in a "bola", a meatball with ground meat, bread and eggs.

SPAIN

Spanish cuisine has always been a mix of the traditional and the innovative. It was the Spanish who introduced the first products from the Americas into their cuisine—potatoes, tomatoes, corn, cacao, and coffee. But the recipes for many of Spain's traditional dishes have been passed down through the centuries intact, including recipes from the country's monasteries.
The coastal cuisine with its spices, vegetables and fresh fish is decidedly more wide-ranging than the food in the poorer inland regions, which is made up of mostly meat and legume dishes.

POTATO TORTILLA

This second course dish is so much richer than your usual omelet. Heat a few spoons of oil in a skillet and add 500 g (1.1 lb) of potatoes and 200 g (7 oz) of thinly sliced onion and cook them until they soften. In the meantime, beat 7 eggs. Season the eggs with salt and pepper and pour them over the vegetables. Cook the omelet till it is set on one side then turn it over and cook it for just a few minutes on the other. It should be soft on the inside. Serve it hot with vegetables and other tapas.

Atlantic Ocean

Canary Islands

11
JAMÓN IBÉRICO PATA NEGRA

Iberian pigs are used to make this exquisite cured ham. Its flavor is both salty and sweet and should be enjoyed unadulterated, with simply a slice of bread.

5
FABADA ASTURIANA

Fabada is the signature dish of the Asturias region. Traditionally made with pork and legumes, it is a very rich dish, perfect for winter.

6
TARTA DE SANTIAGO

This typical Galician almond cake is still offered to the pilgrims along the Santiago path just as it was when it was created in the Middle Ages.

7
CHURROS

Churros batter is piped into boiling oil from a syringe–like tool with a star–shaped nozzle. These fragrant pastries can be eaten with sugar and cinnamon or dipped in hot chocolate sauce.

8
PAPARAJOTES

This refined, fragrant dessert made of battered, fried lemon leaves has its origins in Arab cuisine. The fried leaves are coated in sugar and go well with a glass of anisette.

9
QUESO MANCHEGO

The milk of the Manchego sheep native to the Castile region is used to make this cheese. The Spanish love the pungent, bitter taste it adds to their favorite dishes.

10
ARNADÍ

Valencia's typical Easter dessert resembles a pudding. It is made with squash, eggs and almonds aromatized with lemon and cinnamon. It is customarily eaten with a glass of Muscat.

Marmitako

Tortilla de bacalao

Huevos al salmorejo

Paella

Lechazo

Tocino de cielo

PAELLA

Spain's national dish originated in rural culture, where the few ingredients that were available were cooked together in one iron pan and served for dinner. So it was that rice was combined with vegetables and fish, but with fowl and poultry as well. At the end of the 19th century paella was sold in food stands on the beaches in Valencia and Alicante, and thanks to tourists, it soon made its way to the rest of Spain. The pan used to make paella is called paellera. It is large and shallow with two thin handles.

Mediterranean Sea

12
PISTO CON HUEVO

Pisto is La Mancha's version of French ratatouille. Tomatoes, peppers, zucchini and onions are fried and then simmered until they almost fall apart. This is the recipe with eggs.

13
CATALAN CREAM

A dense, cinnamon scented cream is the base for this world famous pudding. Sugar is sprinkled on its surface and then caramelized into a hard crust using a special scorching hot cast iron grill pan. The result is a hardened, hot crust you will have to break in order to savor this delicious dessert.

14
CANTABRIAN ANCHOVIES

The big, meaty anchovies from the Cantabrian Sea are considered the best in the world. The currents in the Cantabrian make for a rough sea, but they also make for excellent fishing.

15
MANTECADOS DE ESTEPA

In the 16th century, this traditional dessert of Seville was made in the convents of the area using almonds, flour, lard and sugar mixed with an infinity of aromas like cinnamon, coconut, hazelnut and cocoa. The sweets were stored in cardboard boxes that were genuine works of art.

1
SALTED CARAMEL

This tantalizing sauce made with caramel, heavy cream and a pinch of salt from the salt flats of Guérande is the perfect addition to cakes, ice cream or cookies or it can be enjoyed all by itself.

2
BRETON GALETTES

These savory crepes are typical of Brittany. They are made with buckwheat flour and filled with ham, cheese and eggs, and folded into a rectangle.

3
CROISSANT AND VIENNOISERIE

These typical French pastries are made from leavened dough or puff pastry. They can have a variety of fillings including chocolate, cream and raisins or jam and all of them are irresistible.

4
RATATOUILLE

Typically Provençal, this is a dish of stewed summer vegetables aromatized with characteristic Mediterranean herbs.

5
BOUILLABAISSE

This fish stew is cooked over a low flame. The basic recipe calls for 4 types of fish: scorpionfish, red mullet, conger eel and gurnard, but you can also add shellfish and mollusks.

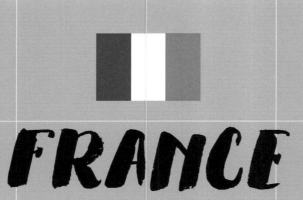

FRANCE

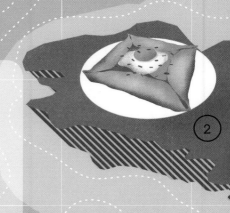

②

From cuisine du terroir (local cuisine) to the more creative nouvelle cuisine, France's culinary traditions encompass an infinite variety of dishes and flavors. There is something for everyone including over 400 kinds of cheese, a multitude of distinguished wines and countless refined desserts. Each region is known for its specialties: Lorraine for its rich quiches, Normandy for its cheeses, Brittany for its fish and shellfish and Provence and the Côte d'Azur for their vegetables and fish, typical of the Mediterranean diet. There is one common thread, though: the use of sauces. Be it aïoli from Marseilles, béchamel, remoulade or Béarnaise, sauce accompanies every dish and it exalts the flavors of the other ingredients and never covers them.

Atlantic Ocean

CREPES

To prepare these thin little omelets, beat 3 eggs with 250 g (2 cups) of flour. Stir in 500 ml (2 cups) of milk, a pinch of salt and, if you are going to use a sweet filling, a tablespoon of sugar. Heat a non–stick skillet over medium heat and grease it with a bit of butter. Ladle a spoonful of the batter into the skillet and shake the pan to distribute the batter evenly. Cook the crepe on each side until it is golden brown, fill it with your favorite filling and then enjoy it while it is hot.

Auguste Escoffier was the first person to go to the trouble of codifying French cuisine, which thanks to him became a point of reference for haute cuisine all over the world. In fact, in 2010, the Gastronomic Meal of the French was declared Intangible Cultural Heritage of Humanity by UNESCO.

The Chef ESCOFFIER

12
COQ AU VIN

Vegetables and Gallic rooster, the symbol of France, dive together into a pot of red wine to make this robust stew, perfect for a cold winter day.

13
SAINT-HONORÉ

Sponge cake covered with cream and chocolate cream piped in flame–shaped rosettes and crowned with cream puffs—who could ask for more?

14
HERBES DE PROVENCE

The codified recipe for this spice mix from Provence says it must contain each of these typical Mediterranean herbs: thyme, rosemary, basil, fennel, sage, marjoram, mint, oregano and summer savory.

15
THE OYSTER FARMERS OF CANCALE

When the tide is out on the bay of Cancale you can see its network of oyster farms dug out of the clay. The farmers can be seen at all hours of the day, in their hip boots and armed with plenty of patience, checking water levels and to see how their oysters are growing. Many of them also have food stands nearby, where you can order a dozen oysters and enjoy them looking out over the bay.

16
CAMEMBERT

Camembert was first produced in the 1600s in the Normandy village of the same name. The cheese, made with raw cow's milk, is soft with a candid white crust and can only be sold in poplar wood boxes.

6
BEIGNETS AND ÉCLAIRS

Pâte à Choux is made with flour and eggs and is used to create these little treasure chests. They can be round or oval and are filled with every possible variation on cream.

7
GREEN OYSTERS FROM LOIRE

These oysters, typical of the Loire region, get their green gills from feeding on a blue diatom that is abundant in the clay ponds they grow in.

8
PAIN D'ÉPICES

A cross between bread and plum cake, this Alsatian Christmas dessert is spiced with green anise, cloves, ginger and cardamom.

9
FOIE GRAS

A notable and quite disputed product of French gastronomy, fois gras is the liver of a goose fattened by force—feeding. It is rich tasting—perfect to spread on a slice of French bread.

10
MACARONS

With a shell made from egg whites, almonds and sugar, these little sweets filled with creams or fruit compotes are known for their flavors as well as for their beautiful soft colors.

11
TARTE TATIN

How could the Tatin sisters have known that a pie filled with caramel covered apples, baked and turned upside down, would become such a worldwide success!

Baguette

Roquefort

Green lentils from Loire

Apples

Mediterranean Sea

1
YORKSHIRE PUDDING

These little fritters are baked in the oven and are usually served with Sunday roast.

2
IRISH MEAT

Irish beef is known the world over for its quality. One of the most successful dishes is beef stew, cooked in Guinness beer that infuses all of its aromas into the beef.

3
COLCANNON

This traditional Irish side dish is made with mashed potatoes and cabbage prepared with milk, butter and pearl onions.

4
PUDDING

Pudding is a word used to designate more than one kind of dessert in England. It can be a simple pudding or a soft dessert made with bread and butter soaked in milk and embellished with all sorts of ingredients, from candied fruit to caramel sauce.

5
ENGLISH DUMPLINGS

When the meat stew is almost ready, these flour and water based dumplings go on top, then the whole dish goes back into the oven to finish baking.

UNITED KINGDOM AND IRELAND

English cuisine has a lot of traditional dishes that are simple but not always particularly appetizing. Over the years, however, it has become a lot richer thanks to the influence of North America and the Indies, ex—colonies of the British Empire. Tradition lives on in roasts and meat dishes—the same ones that are typical of Ireland, home to sheep and cow farms. You may not find a lot of fish on the menu in England, but that is not the case in Ireland, the green isle with the cold but bountiful sea. The covered markets in the little towns scattered along the sea cliffs sell everything you need to make fish and shellfish soups and more.

SCONES

The ingredients you need to make these delightful sweets are: 200 g (20 tbsp) of flour, 20 g (4 tsp) of sugar, 50 g (1/4 cup) of butter and 150 ml (1/2 cup) of milk. Mix the ingredients with a packet of baking powder and let the dough rest in the refrigerator for 15 minutes. Roll out the dough on a floured surface, cut little rounds and bake them on a baking sheet in a 400 °F (200 °C) oven for 15 minutes. Serve with jam or sour cream.

FIVE O' CLOCK TEA

The tradition of five o'clock tea dates back to the 1800s when the English were not in the habit of eating lunch. Every day, in the late afternoon, Anne, the 7th Duchess of Bedford, suffered from strong hunger pangs that made it difficult for her to wait for dinner. To alleviate the pangs, she asked for something "light" to hold her over till meal time and a maid brought tea and biscuits shortly before five. It was not long before the habit caught on in all social classes and today, in homes throughout England, between half past three and five o'clock, you will be served black tea with sugar and milk along with finger sandwiches, scones and cupcakes.

11
CORNISH PASTY

Time ago, meat hash was wrapped in puff pastry to make it easier to eat on the job. Today, it is Cornwall's favorite street food.

12
TRIFLE

The Anglo—Saxons love their layered cream desserts and the trifle is the crowning glory of the category. Pastry cream, merengue and slices of sponge cake are layered with fruit to make these mouthwatering creations.

13
COTTAGE PIE

To make this traditional English beef pie, stewed meat is covered with a soft layer of mashed potatoes and cheese and baked in the oven.

6 CRANACHAN

This is a traditional Scottish dessert. Sugar–covered raspberries on the bottom of a glass are covered with cream, honey and a handful of toasted sugary oat flakes.

Shetland Islands

7 CHEDDAR CHEESE

This hard, orange cheese with its distinctive flavor is omnipresent in English cuisine. It gets its name from its area of origin.

8 HAGGIS

This is the best–known Scottish sausage. Entrails are ground with onions, kidney fat, oat flour, salt and spices, then softened with broth and encased in a sheep's stomach.

North Sea

9 JACKET POTATO

Roll your potatoes in aluminum foil and cook them under the coals. When they are ready, fill them with cheese or bacon or sour cream and enjoy them while they are hot.

10 CRUMBLE

A crumble is a cake made with cooked fruit then covered with crunchy granules made of eggs, flour and butter. With a scoop of ice cream, it makes a perfect snack.

Lobster fishermen

1

HERRING

Herring is the quintessential North Sea fish. It is commonly fried, baked and steamed, but the most typical way of preserving it is in brine with herbs and spices.

2

TØRRFISK

Stockfish, the main source of income for the Lofoten Islands, is exported to the entire world. It is one of the dietary staples of the area's population.

3

PULLA

What do Finnish children eat at snack time? These soft little brioches flavored with cardamom and vanilla with a tall glass of milk, of course!

4

ROSE HIP SOUP

This red Swedish dessert soup is made from rose hips and served hot with almonds and almond cookies.

5

KÖTTBULLAR

These typical Swedish meatballs are simple to make from a mixture of ground beef and pork with milk–soaked bread. They are served with a meat and cream sauce, pickles, mashed potatoes and cranberry jam.

SWEDEN, NORWAY AND FINLAND

Sweden, Norway and Finland have similar culinary cultures, influenced by the maritime trade, which has always been important here, and by the Scandinavian climate, where the temperature is below zero for many months of the year. Fish is obviously a fundamental element of this cuisine—codfish, herring and salmon are on the table on a daily basis. Pork is common, but reindeer, moose and mutton can be found in stews and meatballs. Meals usually begin with a hot soup and a salad to contrast the cold and to fill up on vitamins, while sweets with their fragrance of spices and butter are a favorite at snack time. One example is the famous Swedish Kannelbullar (Cinnamon rolls), a little wheel of leavened dough full of cinnamon and sugar.

CINNAMON ROLLS

Mix 450 g (3 and 1/2 cups) of white flour, 1 teaspoon of cardamom and 7 g (1 tsp) of dry yeast with 250 ml (1 cup) of warm milk, 85 g (slightly more than 1/3 cup) of melted butter and 1 egg. Shape the dough into a ball and after it has had time to rise, roll it out into a rectangle, brush it with melted butter and sprinkle it with sugar and cinnamon. Then roll it up and cut it into 1.5 cm (0.5 in) thick slices. Arrange the slices on a baking sheet and let them rise for another 30 minutes. Bake them in a 400 °F (200 °C) oven for 15 minutes.

Norwegian Sea

(14)

(10)

6

PANNKAKOR

Pippi Longstocking mixed a batter of eggs and flour to make these delectable little Swedish pancakes filled with cream, sugar and berries. Children loved them.

7

LEIPÄJUUSTO

Imagine a pizza made of cheese and cooked under the oven grill until its surface is slightly charred and the cheese melts. Is your mouth watering yet?

8

VALKOSIPULISOPPA

A soup to ward off the vampires, chock full of garlic that the Finnish adore! It has many health benefits, but it is also surprisingly good, especially with croutons and a couple of herring.

9

TISDAGSSOPPA

Made with milk, barley and potatoes, this soup used to be served on Tuesdays, when there was nothing left in the pantry and the fishermen had not yet come back with their first catch of the week.

10

SEMLA

These cardamom–spiced sweet rolls filled with almond paste and topped with whipped cream are perfect with a cup of hot chocolate or as a substitute for lunch.

11

KALAKUKKO

This loaf of rye bread filled with fish and bacon was considered a perfect picnic lunch for woodsmen and farmers or for church worshipers who had a long walk to town to hear Mass.

12

LAKKA

Cloudberries are common to all of the tundra. Their acidic taste makes them a good addition to salads, but they are also eaten as fruit or made into jams and liqueurs.

13

REINDEER MEAT

Reindeer are plentiful in the woods and their meat is used in a number of wild game dishes. Reindeer stew is cooked slowly with spices. It is served with mashed potatoes, cranberry sauce and stewed onions.

14

FALUKORV

Sizzling with flavor, this lightly smoked sausage is wrapped in aluminum foil and cooked directly on the coals. It is a favorite dish to savor in the sauna.

Pepparkakor

Mämmi

Baltic
Sea

SALMON FISHING and GRAVLAX

Fishing is fundamental in Scandinavia and the myriad of fish species that inhabit the region's lakes and rivers and the Baltic Sea guarantee a plentiful catch. Salmon fishing is one of the area's favorites, usually in the spring when the fish swim upstream to the lakes. Salt curing, the method used to make gravlax, and smoking are the best ways to preserve the fish for the longest time. The basic marinade for making gravlax is salt, sugar and dill, but it may be infused with other herbs that vary from region to region. It is a common dish in the Baltic region.

1
SPLIT PEA SOUP

Originally created to feed the soldiers, this dense, creamy soup is made with split peas and vegetables and is customarily served with smoked sausage and black bread with butter and ham.

2
RYE BREAD

White bread is hard to find here, particularly in the countryside where the bread is always either whole wheat or rye—a grain that flourishes in these lands that once belonged to the sea.

3
HERRING

Holland's streets are full of food stands and one of the most popular street foods is grilled herring. Take it by the tail and bite it or ask for it in a sandwich with onion and lots of mustard.

4
CARBONADE FLAMANDE

One of the most famous Flemish dishes in the world, this meat and vegetable stew is cooked in dark beer with thyme and bay leaves. The result is meat that is as black as coal.

5
CHOCOLATE PRALINES

Once again, we have to thank the Belgians for this marvelous treat. They invented the finely wrapped chocolate shells filled with tasty cream that we know today.

6
BRUSSEL SPROUTS

The Brussels sprout plant looks like a miniature tree made of little green balls. In this region the sprouts are served with béchamel sauce and cheese or cooked with bacon and chestnuts.

THE NETHERLANDS, LUXEMBOURG AND BELGIUM

Food in the Netherlands is a blend of countless flavors from other lands—including the Caribbean, whose influence the colonial conquerors brought back with them. The result is a simple, homemade cuisine where the main meal, dinner, is always highly caloric and served very early.

On the other hand, in Belgium, a country with richer origins, the food resembles French cuisine. Unlike in the Netherlands, people enjoy eating at all hours of the day, so snacks and street food are popular.

WAFFLES

Soft on the inside and crispy outside, these waffles are made on a special iron pan; today an electric version is available. They are usually served with a sprinkle of powdered sugar on top, but you will also find them with whipped cream, ice cream, chocolate syrup . . . They are everywhere and their delightful vanilla scent is always in the air. This recipe handed down by local grandmothers calls for 190 g (19 tbsp) of flour with 1 egg, 75 ml (6 tbsp) of milk, 50 g (1/3 cup) of butter, 5 tbsp of sugar granules, a pinch of yeast and 45 g (4 tbsp) of powdered sugar. Let the batter rise for about an hour then ladle it onto the hot iron.

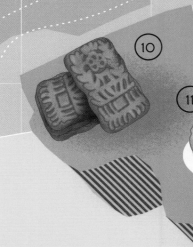

⑩

⑪

9
RICE CAKE

A humble dessert typical in all of central Europe, a rice cake is a shortbread crust filled with a very sweet rice and milk pudding.

10
SPECULOOS

These crispy little cookies with cinnamon and caramel are usually served with coffee.

11
BREAD CAKE

This homemade cake is made with eggs, butter, milk, dried bread, raisins and not much else.

12
MUSSELS AND MOLLUSKS

Steamed mussels are a favorite in the Netherlands, while the Belgians prefer "moules et frittes", mussels cooked in a sauce of garlic and parsley and served in a large casserole with a huge portion of Belgian frites on the side.

13
KROKET

This Dutch street food was originally created to recycle leftovers, mostly meat but nowadays fish, shrimp and vegetable croquettes are available as well.

7
MIMOLETTE

The particularity of this cheese is that it is round and . . . orange! Its color comes from adding annatto, a spice native to the Amazon rainforest.

8
STROOPWAFEL

This is the land of the waffle. The stroopwafel is ultrathin and usually made up of two waffles with a layer of toffee in the middle.

North Sea

Eels

Belgian endive

BELGIAN FRITES

Belgian frites are a source of pride and joy for the Belgians. The potatoes are peeled, left in water to remove their starch and dried with care. They are fried for a first time, drained, left to cool and then fried again in boiling oil. That is the only way to achieve Belgian frites that are crispy outside and tender inside.

14
PIG FARMING

No part of this animal is thrown away. The rind is cooked with legumes, the meat is stewed or roasted and the feet are used to make sausage. Even the milk has its use—someone has come up with the idea of cheese made from sow's milk.

15
POFFERTJES

You will find these thick, sweet pancakes at breakfast with a dusting of powdered sugar.

16
TRAPPIST BEER

Who makes this world famous beer? The Trappist monks do. This kind of beer is produced in 12 monastery breweries, 6 of which are in Belgium.

1
GERMAN GOULASH

The German version of this Hungarian stew is made with veal, an abundance of peppers and a bit of tomato, none of which are used in the original version.

2
PRETZEL

This famous twisted bread with salt granules originated in the monasteries of the 1600s as a way to utilize left over bread. Its twisted form was meant to be reminiscent of arms folded in prayer and the three holes symbolized the Holy Trinity. The dough is boiled for a few seconds in water and baking soda before baking it to give it its traditional shiny brown color.

3
KRAPFEN

These sweets are made with fried leavened dough and are filled with cream or jam. During carnival, they are covered in sugar before they are devoured.

4
LINZER TORTE

This pie is typical in the area of Linz. Its shortbread crust has hazelnuts and cinnamon and its filling is made with red berry jam.

5
BLACK FOREST CAKE

This chocolate dessert oozes cream and sour cherries from its brandy drenched sponge cake layers. It is typical of the mountainous region of Freiburg.

North Sea

GERMANY

German cuisine was heavily influenced by the austere, military–like culture of the Prussians. This influence is still evident today in the widespread consumption of potatoes, pork, sauerkraut, soups, peas and meatballs, all meager dishes made with readily available ingredients. Despite this fact, every Lander (region) has developed its own specialty. Throughout most of the country, a typical meal consists of a meat–based main dish (the small amount of fish consumed here is eaten mostly in the northern regions) with salad and cooked vegetables and ends with one of many traditional desserts.

CURRYWURST

This typical street food belongs to a modern, cosmopolitan German cuisine. To make the sauce, sauté a thinly sliced onion in 2 tbsp of oil, add mild paprika, smoked paprika, 4 tbsp of curry powder, cumin and 250 g (1 cup) of tomato sauce and cook the sauce till it thickens. Then add 150 g (2/3 cup) of ketchup. Put a generous amount of this sauce on your favorite grilled sausage and serve it with French fries.

Not just HOT DOGS!

Pork is a prevalent ingredient in German cuisine and even though you might find a pork roast on the table, processed meat products are more popular. The famous hot dog is an example of how well–loved sausages are, but it is not just all about hot dogs. Sausages can be enriched with entrails, pig's blood, liver and rind as well as some less noble parts of the animal that in any case do not deserve to end up in the garbage. Ham hocks are also a common dish, roasted or in a vinegar sauce and served with a nice potato salad and a bit of sauerkraut.

9
DAMPFNUDELN

The Palatinate region is home to these sweet miniature loaves of leavened dough that are steam cooked and served with vanilla cream or zabaione.

10
LEBKUCHEN FROM NUREMBERG

This gingerbread cookie has candied lemon, cloves, anise, cinnamon and cardamom and is frosted with beautiful drawings. It is most commonly served around Christmas.

11
KÄSEKUCHEN

Quark, a cheese made with fermented milk and cream, is the base for this baked, cheesecake–like dessert, commonly found in Europe.

12
SAUERKRAUT

Thinly sliced cabbage left to ferment in vinegar produces one of the most popular foods in Germany, eaten either as a side dish or in soup.

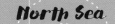

6 GUGELHUPF

A cloud of leavened almond paste, this doughnut shaped treat is a Christmas tradition. Some recipes also call for raisins and candied fruit.

7 FLAMMKUCHEN

It is almost a pizza. Cooked in a wood burning oven and covered with bacon, onions and cream, this delight can only be found in the region bordering Alsace.

8 PRÜGELTORTE

Even though this sweet originated in Austria, it is commonly served in Germany's border region too. Dough made with eggs, butter and sugar is cooked on a spit that turns over an open fire. It tastes a little like shortbread cookies.

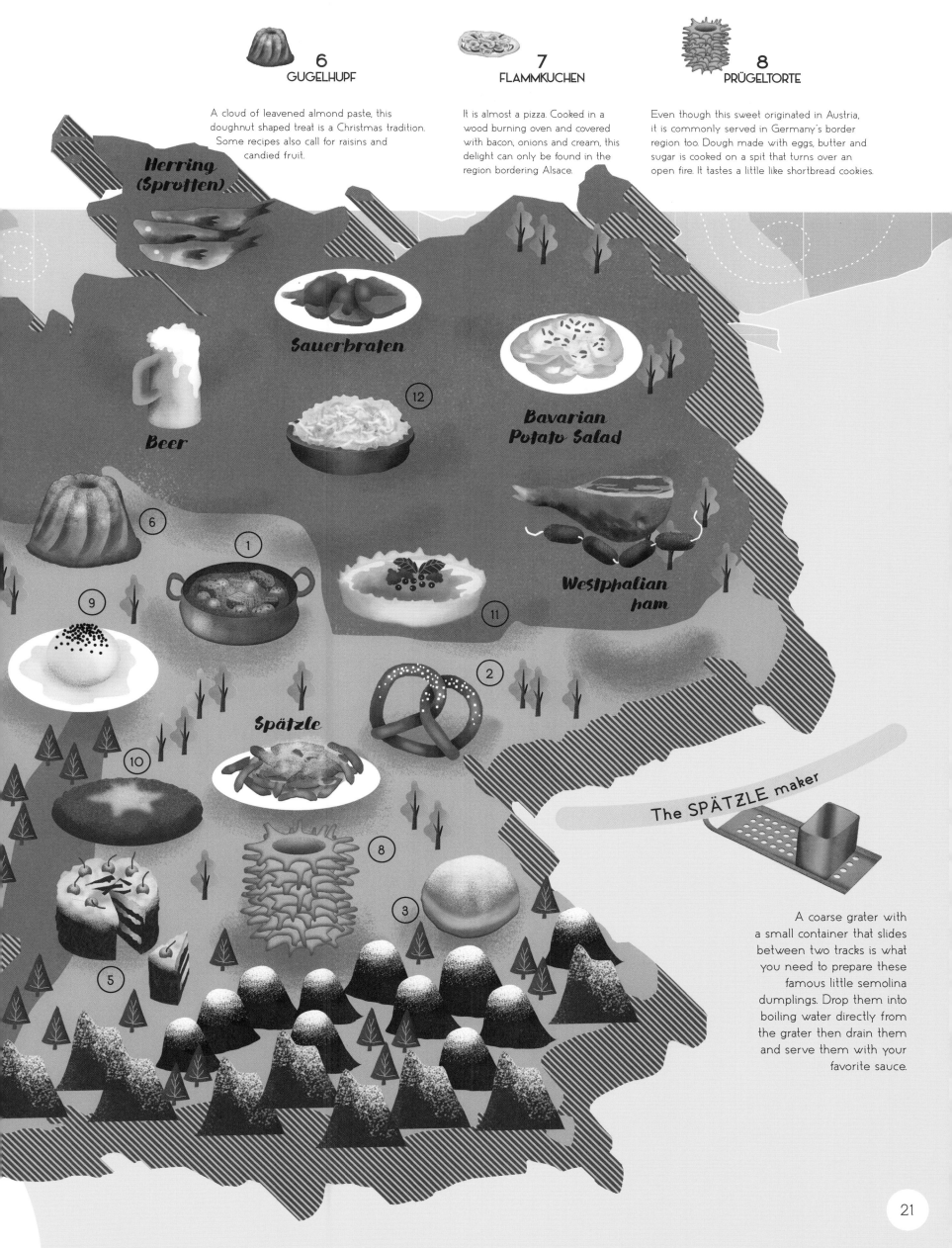

The SPÄTZLE maker

A coarse grater with a small container that slides between two tracks is what you need to prepare these famous little semolina dumplings. Drop them into boiling water directly from the grater then drain them and serve them with your favorite sauce.

1 MAKOWIEC

A filling with poppy seeds, butter, raisins and almonds is wrapped in a fragrant, leavened dough. It is commonly served during winter holidays.

2 CEBULARZ LUBELSKI

This is the only bread to have the European Union's protection. Its origins are Jewish and it is still prepared today in the city of Lublin. A base of slightly sweet dough in the shape of a pizza is covered with raw onion mixed with poppy seeds.

3 PIEROGI

Fry or boil these little dumplings and serve them with butter, sour cream and poppy seeds. They are perfect for an appetizer and you will often see them on holiday tables in Poland.

4 CARP

The queen (fish) of the Polish table is carp: fried, cooked in gelatin or boiled.

5 TROUT FARMERS

In the last few years trout consumption has increased so much in Poland that the country is now the fifth in Europe for number of trout farms.

POLAND

Polish people have always worked magic in the kitchen—turning poor local ingredients like beets, cabbage, parsnips and sauerkraut into fabulous dishes. But the marks left by the various populations that have lived in the territory make it difficult to characterize Polish cuisine. German, French, Jewish and Italian influences are all evident.
Potatoes are the biggest staple in Poland's diet. They often substitute bread and grains and are the base for soups, creams, first courses, side dishes and even desserts. In other words, no meal would be complete without them!

BARSZCZ

Barszcz is a traditional Christmas Eve soup made with beets. Clean 3 fresh beets and boil them together with 2 carrots, garlic, a bay leaf, salt, pepper, sugar, summer savory, lemon juice and 2 tbsp of vinegar. If you like, you can add a potato. When the vegetables are cooked, blend them together and serve the soup hot with a spoonful of sour cream and uszka, dumplings with meat or mushrooms.

BAGEL

These doughnut-shaped sandwich rolls that have become so popular in the United States actually originated in Poland. They are cooked in a peculiar way: first boiled, then baked in the oven till they become golden brown. Try them with cream cheese, vegetables and cold cuts.

9 GOŁĄBKI

Rice and meat filling is wrapped in cabbage leaves and stewed. Enjoy it with mashed potatoes or the rye bread that is typical to the area.

10 ZAPIEKANKA

Poland's most popular street food, this long thin loaf of bread is cut in half, covered with cheese and mushrooms, baked in the oven and served very hot.

11 PYZY

These are no ordinary potato dumplings! They are enormous round dumplings filled with meat and generally served with melted butter.

12 PĄCZKI

These sweets were traditionally prepared for Fat Thursday, the last Thursday before Lent. Sweet, golden balls of leavened dough covered with sugar and filled with rose jam.

13 SAUSAGES

Polish people love sausages: they are stomach warming in the winter, when the temperature goes below zero, and the number of varieties is countless.

14 SOUR CREAM

It is the result of adding a drop of lemon to the fat obtained from milk, making it curdle slightly. Its bold flavor makes it perfect in savory dishes.

22

6
KROKIETY

Imagine a thin pancake, like a crepe, filled with ground meat and sauerkraut, then breaded and fried. It may not be the lightest dish in the world, but it certainly is very inviting.

7
CHŁODNIK

This soup is as beautiful as it is good! Bright pink with white spots of sour cream and green clumps of chives on top. Beets are the main ingredient.

8
BIGOS

Bigos is Poland's most famous dish. Cabbage, sauerkraut and prunes are added to this slow—cooked meat stew that is served in a bowl made of a hollowed out loaf of bread.

Baltic Sea

Potatoes

1
SOUPS

The most comforting and tasty way to begin your meal in Prague or to make a nourishing dinner is a good hot soup. Soups here are prepared with onions, sauerkraut, sour cream, mushrooms and vegetables or with meat—something for everyone. In some places, soup is served in a hollowed out loaf of bread.

2
GOULASH

This beef stew is completely different than the one you will find in Hungary. It is only mildly hot and spicy and is served as a one–pot meal one with knedliky.

3
SMAŽENÝ SÝR

Stretch cheese between two slices of bread is dipped in egg and milk and then fried and served with hot sauce.

4
CARAWAY

One of the spices used to aromatize pork, its scientific name is *Carum carvi*. Its leaves resemble carrot leaves and its fruit has a pungent flavor similar to anise.

Poppy seeds are found in the poppy plant's ripe seed pods. They are frequently used both in sweets and as a condiment for savory dishes. These seeds were originally introduced by the Celts who even used them in baby food. They favored them for their lightly sedative properties.

POPPY seeds

Mushrooms

5
PRAGUE HAM

The aromas used to season this ham combined with a particular smoking process produce a very different flavor from other types of ham. Steam cooking makes it lighter.

6
OBLOŽENÉ CHLEBÍČKY

Slices of soft bread filled with salmon, ham, eggs, roast beef and cheese with mayonnaise and pickles. These open–faced sandwiches are commonly enjoyed as street food.

7
ROAST PORK

As in most Middle–Europe regions, Sunday roast is a pork roast served with mashed potatoes, cream and meat sauce and cranberry compote.

8
KNEDLÍKY

Cured meats, cheese and vegetables give flavor to these dumplings made with day–old bread. You can find them in soups, covered with cheese, in broth or sautéed in butter. Here, bread dumplings are spindle–shaped, whereas in Germany and Austria they are round.

CZECH REPUBLIC

The country's geographical position and its history have both influenced Czech cuisine, which clearly reflects the proximity of Germany and Austria. But the Bohemia region, the most important region in the country and home to the capital, has developed its own gastronomy thanks to the abundance of agricultural resources (every imaginable vegetable grows here) and to the successful breeding of lambs and pigs that is common in the area. The main meal is eaten at noon and snacks throughout the day but evening meals are light: soup and vegetables, with very little meat.
The flavors are bold and spices, garlic, vinegar and cream are used in abundance. What is not popular here is the spicy hot flavor that nearby Hungary loves.

APPLE STRUDEL

Apple strudel is made here too and, apparently, it is one of the best in all of Europe. Cut 3 or 4 rennet apples into cubes and sauté them with a bit of butter, raisins, a spoonful of rum, pine nuts and walnuts. While the filling is cooling, make the dough with 200 g (20 tbsp) of flour and 100 g (8 tbsp) of water. Roll it out till it is as thin as a bride's veil, then grease it with oil, sprinkle it with bread crumbs, spread the filling down the middle and roll it up. Bake it in a 350 °F (180 °C) oven until it is golden brown.

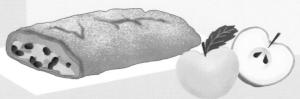

9
UTOPENEC

This plate of pickled sausage and onions is one of the Czechs' favorite afternoon snacks. It is commonly eaten as street food, but you can also order it in your favorite bar along with a glass of beer.

10
ROHLÍKY

You can find these banana-shaped bread rolls on the table at every meal.

11
PASTA

Here, pasta—like rice and other grains—is used as a side dish for roasted meat!

12
PIVNÍ SÝR

It is a beer—marinated cheese to enjoy on a slice of black bread covered in stewed onions.

25

1

DOBOS TORTE

Imagine six layers of sponge cake filled with butter and chocolate cream with sumptuous, shiny, caramel coated bricks on top. This cake was invented by the pastry chef that it is named after in 1884, when there were no refrigerators and the caramel served as an insulant to keep the cake fresher for a longer period of time.

2

GALUSKA

Little semolina dumplings are dropped into water directly from the special grater used to prepare them. They are served with meat stews after having been drenched in butter and cream.

3

BEJGLI

Coiled up like a big snake, this long brioche is filled with chopped walnuts, raisins, sugar and lemon zest or with poppy seeds.

4

PALACSINTA OR HUNGARIAN PANCAKES

Milk and eggs are the base for these thin little fritters. Fill them with fruit or jam or with a savory filling of spicy meat and cream for a tasty lunch.

5

HAJDÚ-BIHAR HORSERADISH

One of Hungary's PDO products, this hot, pungent root is ground together with bread and vinegar to obtain a well-loved condiment for meat and vegetables.

HUNGARY

There is nothing light about Hungarian cuisine—neither the condiments nor the tastes. Every flavor is magnified: spicy, sweet and sour, hot. Everything is intense and determined. And exquisitely memorable. Typical, traditional dishes stem from a rural culture, but also from the times of the empire. You can find dishes derived from Italian cuisine but French, Turkish, English and German influences are also evident. Sour cream, paprika, meat and onions are a part of almost every Hungarian meal, particularly at lunch (*ebéd*), which is still considered the main meal of the day and always ends with a traditional, satiating dessert.

HUNGARIAN GOULASH

If you want to feel like the farmers from the Puszta taking their wares to the market in Vienna, make yourself some of the goulash they used to prepare on an open fire at their campsites. To make this spicy soup, sauté a few thinly sliced onions with veal cubes. Add a lot of paprika, a pepper and some cubed potatoes and cover it all with broth. Let the soup cook for approximately an hour, until it becomes dense and the meat is tender. Season it with salt and serve it with toasted bread and a tablespoon of sour cream.

PAPRIKA

Paprika is the king of spices in Hungarian cuisine. Copious amounts of this magical powder account for the red color of the dishes you will find here—it is not tomato.

Paprika comes from a pepper with its seed and stem removed and left to dry. The pepper is then ground into powder that is mild, never hot. Legend narrates that it was a young Hungarian woman, betrothed to a Turkish pasha, that discovered how to make the spice after having secretly spied on the workers in the gardens of Buda.

Adriatic Sea

6
FISHERMAN'S BROTH

On Christmas Eve, all kinds of fish from Hungary's big lakes (carp, pike, catfish, etc) are cooked together with spices, onions, peppers and potatoes in a broth reddened with paprika.

7
SALÁTA

The vegetables on this platter are pickled to preserve them for the winter and are usually served with beer as an appetizer.

8
SOUPS

There is nothing better than a good hot vegetable soup to help you face Hungarian winters. Vegetables of every kind combine with meat and fish to make a decidedly nourishing first course. Some of the most popular are cabbage soup, mushroom and cream soup and, a favorite with the adults, wine soup. One of the most peculiar, though, is sour cherry soup, served only in the spring.

9
TEJFÖL

Tejföl is Hungary's version of sour cream. The cream is fermented with bacteria resulting in a product similar to compact yogurt but with a milder, rounder flavor.

10
ZSERBÓ SZELET

One of Hungary's favorite desserts was created by a French pastry chef over 100 years ago. This layered cake has an apricot jam and nut filling and is covered in chocolate.

Hungarian salami

Hungarian chestnuts

How to make a good KÜRTŐSKALÁCS dessert

The ritual and the instrument used to make this dessert may be even more special than the dessert itself. Picture a long wooden skewer of about 10 cm (4 in) with a thin ribbon of leavened dough wrapped around it. The skewered dough is dipped in sugar and cinnamon and put to bake over burning coals. As the dough cooks, the sugar caramelizes and forms a sweet crust. When the chimney shaped pastry is cooked it can be topped with chocolate cream, almonds, jam or any other sweet frosting that pleases you.

11
ONION

It is impossible to think of Hungarian cuisine without thinking of onions. If you would like to grow some of your own to add to your goulash, put the end of a cut onion on some humid soil. In a few days, you will see the first green sprouts and a couple of months later you can harvest your first crop.

12
RÁKÓCZI TÚRÓS

From a short crust pastry base, a mountain of sweet Hungarian ricotta rises up to meet a layer of jam and a merengue topping. This delight was first created in the early 1900s by one of Hungary's most famous chefs.

13
SOMLÓI GALUSKA

Sponge cake and vanilla cream drenched in chocolate syrup and topped with whipped cream is undoubtedly one of the best things ever to end a meal.

1
PIEDMONT HAZELNUTS

Round and mild (Tonda Gentile) just as their name suggests, the hazelnuts from the areas of Cuneo, Asti and Alessandria are used in countless preparations.

2
BITTO AND PIZZOCCHERI

The Valtellina valley is home to Italy's buckwheat production and to this typical tagliatelle pasta dish served with local cheese, such as bitto, casera and a lot of butter!

3
FONTINA VAL D'AOSTA

When the cows are allowed to graze on the alpine pastures, the milk they produce is even tastier. The dairymen from the Aosta Valley use their experience to transform that milk into this famous cheese.

4
FRICO

To make frico you will need potatoes, an onion and lots and lots and lots of Montasio cheese. Cook them together in a frying pan—you will get a fantastic omelet-like dish. Try not to overdo it!

Apples from Trentino

ITALY

Throughout the world, Italy is the epitome of good food. Every day, the thousands of large and small manufacturers scattered over the country work their magic with select raw materials that are prevalently Italian. From the cheeses of the Alps to the great variety of wheat produced in southern Italy and from the cured meats of Umbria and Tuscany to the dishes prepared with the fish carefully and respectfully caught along the coasts of the peninsula, Italy has it all.

Following the traditional recipes that the great chef Pellegrino Artusi classified for the first time, home cooks and chefs alike transform all these specialties into the unique and beloved dishes that the whole world tries to emulate. Tagliatelle with ragout, pizza, ice cream, flatbread and a host of other delicacies were born in Italy.

Tomato porridge

SPAGHETTI with tomato sauce

It is not difficult to make a good tomato sauce to serve with your favorite pasta (in Italy there are more than 130 different types, but the most typical is spaghetti!).

Make a small incision in the skin of some ripe tomatoes and blanch them in boiling water to make them easier to peel. Heat a bit of oil in a skillet and sauté a thinly sliced onion. Mash the peeled tomatoes by hand and add them to the onion along with a teaspoon of sugar and a pinch of salt. Cook the sauce over low heat until it thickens. Add some chopped fresh basil and a handful of grated Parmesan cheese and then, run to the table!

In the past, and still today in the south, families made their own tomato puree to keep for the winter months. It was a ritual, a party that marked the end of summer and the moment to begin storing up provisions for the more difficult months to come—an attempt to bottle up not only tomatoes, but the wonderful smells of the most generous season.

Mirto

12
SARDINIAN SEADAS

These little treasure chests of fried dough have a cheesy center and a honey coating. Need I say more to explain how delicious they are?

13
CHILI PEPPERS FROM SOVERATO

This ultra-hot chili pepper has made Calabria famous. It is used to make some of the region's specialties like 'nduja or bomba, a hot sauce for dipping or spreading.

14
WHEAT AND PASTA

Senatore Cappelli, Timillia and Solina are just a few of the many varieties of wheat that grow in the Apulia region and throughout all of southern Italy. The wheat is transformed into flour to use in bread, flat breads and pasta.

15
CASTELLUCCIO LENTILS

The area around Norcia is famous for more than its cured meats. At the beginning of the summer, these lentils paint the countryside with their flowers and in winter, they warm up the cold days in robust soups.

16
MOZZARELLA

For over 1,100 years buffalo milk has been used in this area to produce mozzarella, a stretched-curd cheese, pinched off by hand and shaped into balls or braids. One of the best loved cheeses in the country.

5
PIADINA

A thin disc of dough made with flour and lard is cooked on a double–edged flat grill pan, patented for this purpose. The most traditional flatbread is filled with fresh cream cheese and prosciutto.

6
LIGURIAN PESTO

The best pesto comes from Liguria; made with garlic from Vessalico, basil from Pra, pecorino and parmesan cheese and pine nuts ground together by hand in a mortar and mixed with olive oil.

7
TORTELLINI

It is said that perfect tortellini are the size of the tip of your pinky finger and resemble the navel of Venus. The best are those that are masterfully prepared by the homemakers of the Romagna region.

8
MATERA BREAD

Only durum wheat, natural yeast and water go into this pale yellow bread. It is shaped into a long thin loaf folded in two and baked in a wood burning oven, just like it has been for centuries.

9
EXTRA VIRGIN OLIVE OIL

Olive groves are everywhere in Italy: from Lake Garda to Lake Como, throughout Liguria and Tuscany and all the way down to Apulia, Calabria and Sicily, every region makes its own characteristic oil.

10
RIBOLLITA

Do not throw away that old bread. Add it to vegetables, beans and some good pecorino cheese to prepare one of Tuscany's many soups, good in any season.

11
FERRATELLE

The recipe for these sweet waffles is passed down from mother to daughter. The waffles are cooked on a specially made iron that is heated on the fire. Ice cream or jam are the perfect complement.

Coppia ferrarese

Ciauscolo

Adriatic Sea

L'Aquila Saffron

Carbonara

Pizza is the symbol of Italy in the whole world. Dough made with water and flour with a pinch of yeast is left to rest for a long time and then rolled out into delicious rounds and covered with tomato sauce, mozzarella cheese and anything else your imagination can conjure. The pizza is cooked for a short time in a fiery hot oven, preferably wood burning. The master of this art is the pizza chef, whose experience makes it possible to perfectly execute every step and prepare a light tasty pizza, just like the first ones prepared by Raffaele Esposito in Naples in 1889 in honor of Queen Margherita.

PIZZA chef

Focaccia bread from Bari

Ionian Sea

'Nduja

Capers from Pantelleria

Little cassata and cannoli siciliani

Pomodori Pachino

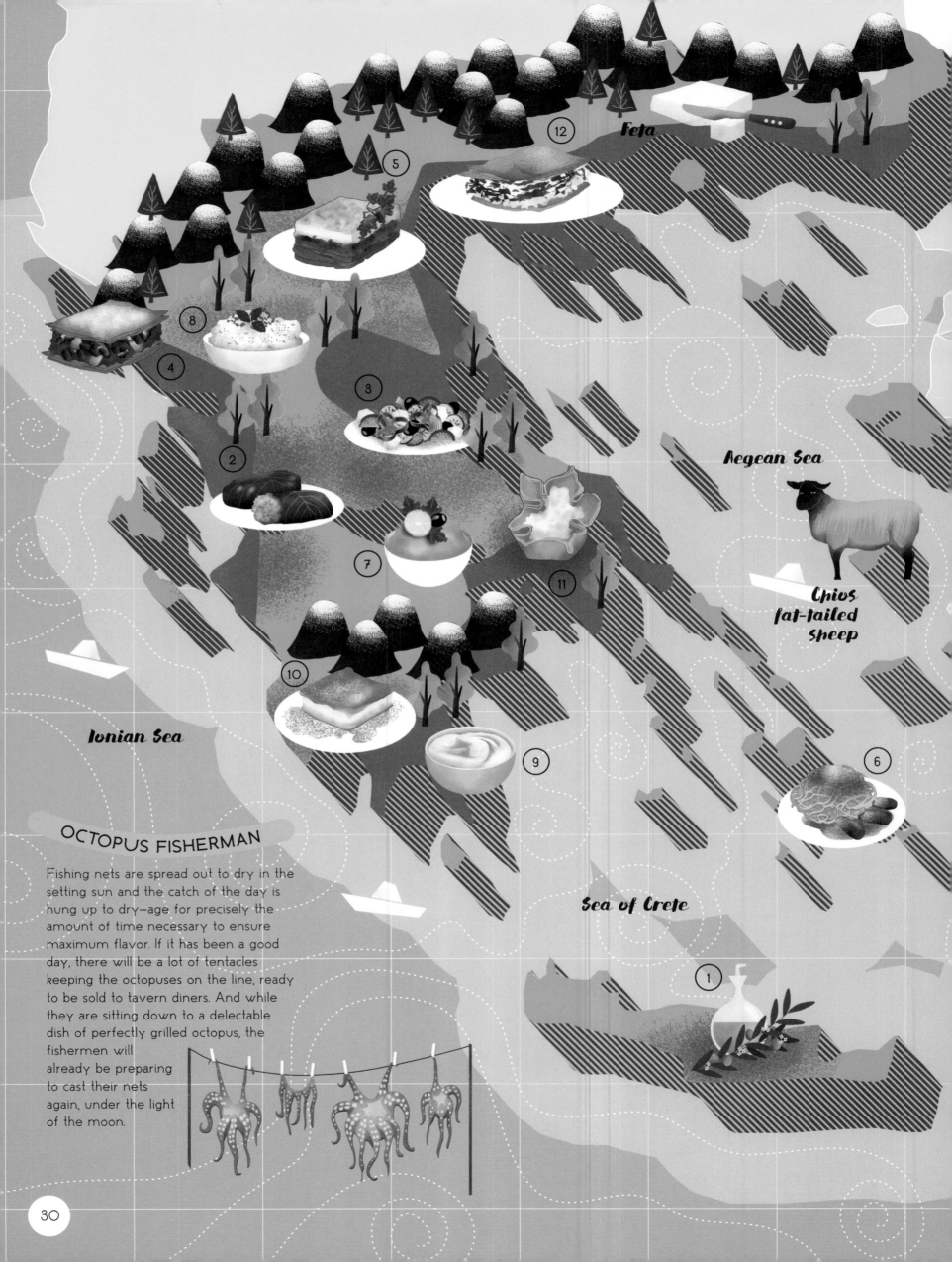

Feta

Aegean Sea

Chios
fat-tailed
Sheep

Ionian Sea

Sea of Crete

OCTOPUS FISHERMAN

Fishing nets are spread out to dry in the setting sun and the catch of the day is hung up to dry-age for precisely the amount of time necessary to ensure maximum flavor. If it has been a good day, there will be a lot of tentacles keeping the octopuses on the line, ready to be sold to tavern diners. And while they are sitting down to a delectable dish of perfectly grilled octopus, the fishermen will already be preparing to cast their nets again, under the light of the moon.

1
EXTRA VIRGIN OLIVE OIL

The entire peninsula produces oil. Together with southern Italy, Greece is probably the biggest producer and exporter of this liquid gold. The best oil comes from the small, dark Kalamata olives—handpicked and cold pressed to guarantee excellence.

2
DOLMADES

Grapes are not the only good thing to eat on the grapevine, the leaves are good too. Preserved in brine, they become a wrap to fill with a traditional rice or meat mix.

3
CHORIATIKI

It is the most famous Greek salad: tomatoes, black olives, feta cheese, onion and oregano come together in a tasty and refreshing dish to enjoy during Greece's long hot summers.

4
SICOMADA

This cake is typical of Corfu. Its base is a fragrant, nourishing mix of dried figs, walnuts, almonds, cinnamon, cloves, nutmeg, orange peel, grape must and ouzo.

5
MOUSSAKA

Eggplant, ragout and béchamel are the main ingredients in this wholesome, tasty casserole. Every household has its own secret recipe.

6
MATSATA

On the island of Folegandros, this dish of wheat pasta with tomato sauce and little meatballs is perfect after a rough day at sea.

7
TARAMOSALATA

Brined fish eggs, mostly from carp or codfish, are mixed with lemon, onions, garlic and olives to make a flavorful spread to eat on bread with cucumbers and tomatoes.

8
TZATZIKI

Mashed and drained cucumbers join yogurt, lemon, garlic and mint in this refreshing and tasty sauce.

9
GIAOÙRTI

Giaoùrti, a dense, compact, cheese—like yogurt, is usually served with honey and walnuts for dessert or at snack time.

GREECE

Cooking has always been considered a serious business in Greece. You had to go to school to become a cook in ancient Greece, just like you would today. And gastronomy had its own goddess: Adephagia.

Even today, Greeks love to sit around the table together. A typical meal starts with an array of little appetizers, the mezedes, which are the representation of all of Greece's culinary achievements throughout the centuries. The choices are ample and vary slightly from the continent to the islands, where fish reigns supreme.

SAGANÀKI

A quick but delicious appetizer. Use only the best feta, a sheep's milk cheese that has been made with the same recipe for over 6,000 years. Cut the feta in 5 cm (2 in) cubes, dip them in flour, then, alternately in an egg bath and bread crumbs twice. Fry the cubes in boiling oil and eat them while they are hot.

12
SPANAKOPITA

It takes mastery to roll all those sheets of ultrathin phyllo dough into a narrow spiral and fill it with spinach and cheese. Tiropita, an even more indulgent version of spanakopita, is a dairy lover's dream with its feta and egg filling.

11
PHYLLO DOUGH

You can use these ultrathin sheets of dough made from just water and flour to make spectacular sweet or savory dishes. They originally came to Greece from nearby Turkey.

10
GALAKTOBOUREKO

Only orange and lemon zest add fragrance to this traditional semolina custard wrapped in a treasure chest of countless sheets of phyllo dough.

ASIA

FOOD FOR THE SOUL WITH THE COLORS AND FRAGRANCES OF A RICH ARRAY OF SPICES.

Asian cuisine is a mosaic of countless minuscule tiles—colors and aromas and flavors from the enormous territory that goes from the freezing Siberian steppes to the steaming islets of Thailand, across the vast and colorful lands of India to the Middle East, with all of its nuances.

Middle Eastern customs and traditions resemble more those of North Africa than of those of the rest of Asia. The mixture of religions that exist in this small area make eating a moment of ritual. The foods that can be eaten are dictated by the Bible and the Qur'an and are prepared according to strict rules that ban foods that are considered impure. Holidays and periods of fasting mark the passing of each month. No one uses cutlery; large trays of food are placed in the center of the table and diners use their hands and a piece of unleavened bread to serve themselves.

The rest of the continent is what is known in the Western world as the Orient. It was the destination of commercial routes in the era of the Maritime Republics and a source of spices, teas and culture for the West for many years.

It is difficult to find common ground in such a multitude of dishes, but rice is the one food at the base of almost all of these populations and their cuisines. It is never in excess and it is considered an important means of staying healthy. Precise dietary rules make each dish, in all of its colors and flavors, something almost therapeutic, in the harmony and balance of the energy that it transmits to the body.

TURKEY
page 34

LEBANON
page 38

ISRAEL
page 40

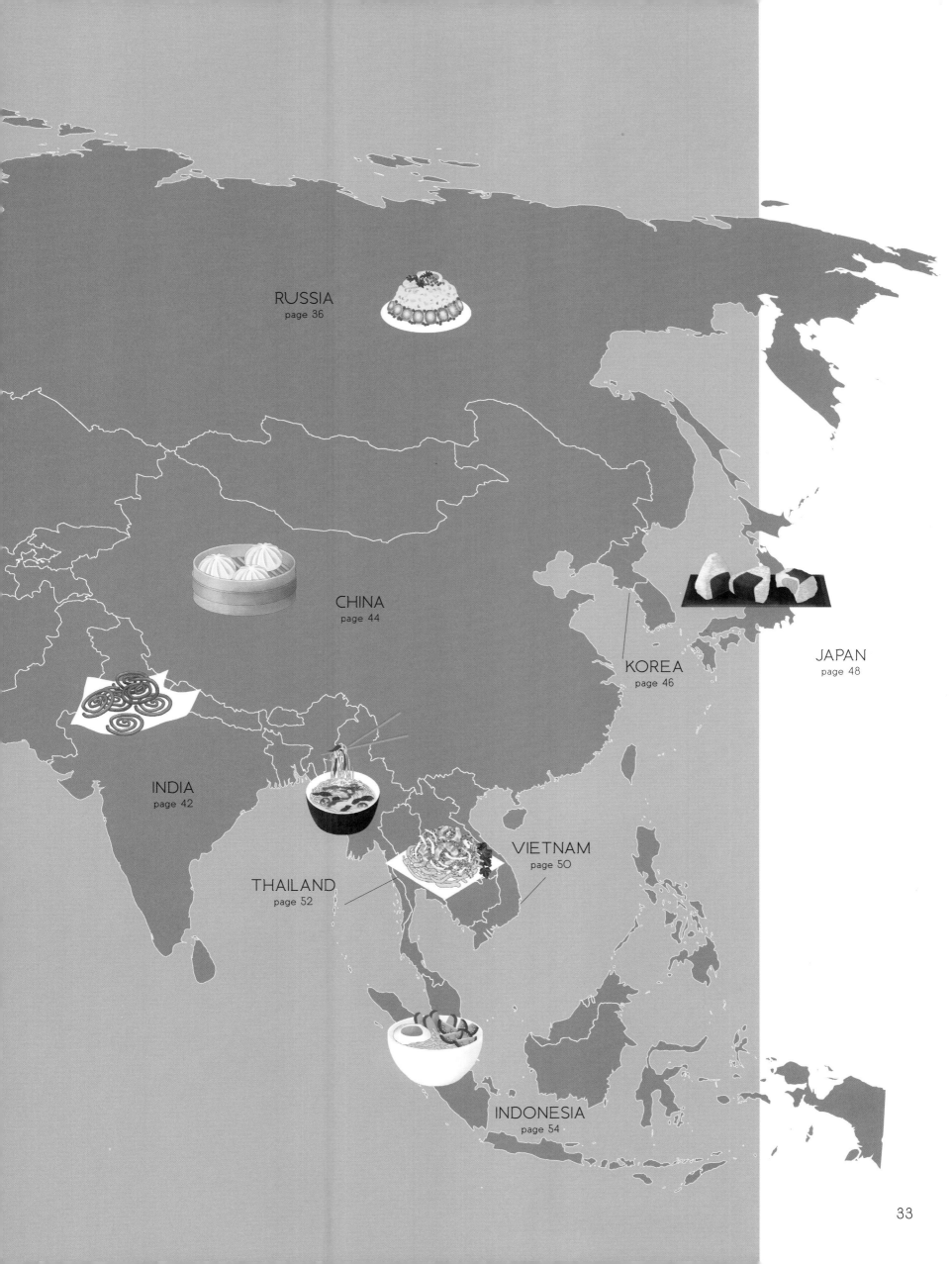

RUSSIA
page 36

CHINA
page 44

KOREA
page 46

JAPAN
page 48

INDIA
page 42

VIETNAM
page 50

THAILAND
page 52

INDONESIA
page 54

TURKEY

Turkey has always been a crossroads of populations, traditions and cultures. On the Mediterranean, between Asia and Europe, and divided between two religions, Turkey has successfully created a balanced mix of its peoples and their traditions. The result is a cuisine that is extraordinarily rich in flavors and spices and tied to the conviviality of eating together. An endless variety of spices are used in savory dishes but also in pastries, where together with nuts and generous doses of sugar and honey, they become sweet, delicious desserts.

RICE PILAF

Almost every Turkish dish is served with rice pilaf. Making it is easy: put long grained rice in a pot, cover it with water and add a cinnamon stick. Cook the rice until all of the water is absorbed, then salt it and serve it with meat stews or soups.

13 GÜLLAÇ

This dessert is made with thin layers of dough soaked in milk and rose water layered with nuts and then covered with pomegranate seeds.

12 SHISH KEBAP

During the period of transhumance, the seasonal migration of livestock, meals were eaten by Turkish nomad populations around a fire with a slow turning spit. Today, these skewers with small cubes of meat are cooked on the grill pan at home and from there, they have conquered the world.

1
BÖREK

Besides being one of the most common dishes in Turkey, it is also the most versatile. To make börek, a very thin sheet of yufka, puff pastry, is filled and cooked on a grill pan. The fillings may be savory or sweet, with meat or nuts and dried fruit. And it can be made in many shapes, depending on how the dough is folded. Sigara böreği, for example, is rolled up into a cigar shape, typically filled with cheese.

2
SIMIT

This bread doughnut covered with sesame seeds is crispy outside and soft inside. It is a favorite breakfast food served with labneh cheese.

3
MANTI

Pasta is a commonplace dish in Turkey, both dried and fresh, such as manti. These tortellini-shaped dumplings are filled with meat, parsley and onions and served with yogurt, garlic and butter.

4
LAHMACUN

This specialty is made with a pizza-like base covered with ground meat, folded in half and baked with tomato and an array of spices. It is commonly eaten as a snack before lunch.

5
KAŞAR

Sheep farms are all over Turkey and this sheep cheese is one of the most widely consumed. It is slightly aged and has a rich, persistent flavor.

6
TULUM

This is another sheep cheese with a peculiarity: it is preserved in sacks of animal origin (sheep stomach or bladder, generally).

7
SOUPS

Turkish meals usually begin with a soup that may or may not be vegetable based. One of the best loved soups is made with lentils and yogurt.

8
SALEP

Salep is a hot, dense winter beverage made with the flour extracted from a particular type of orchid and lots of cinnamon.

TURKISH COFFEE

Very finely ground coffee is added directly to hot water to make Turkish coffee. Before you drink it, make sure that the powder has settled to the bottom. When you are finished, turn the cup over on its saucer and the grounds will run slowly down the inside of the cup, leaving patterns and shapes. Antique instruments playing a musical accompaniment or voices singing old lullabies help create the best atmosphere for reading the signs and telling your future.

Dead Sea

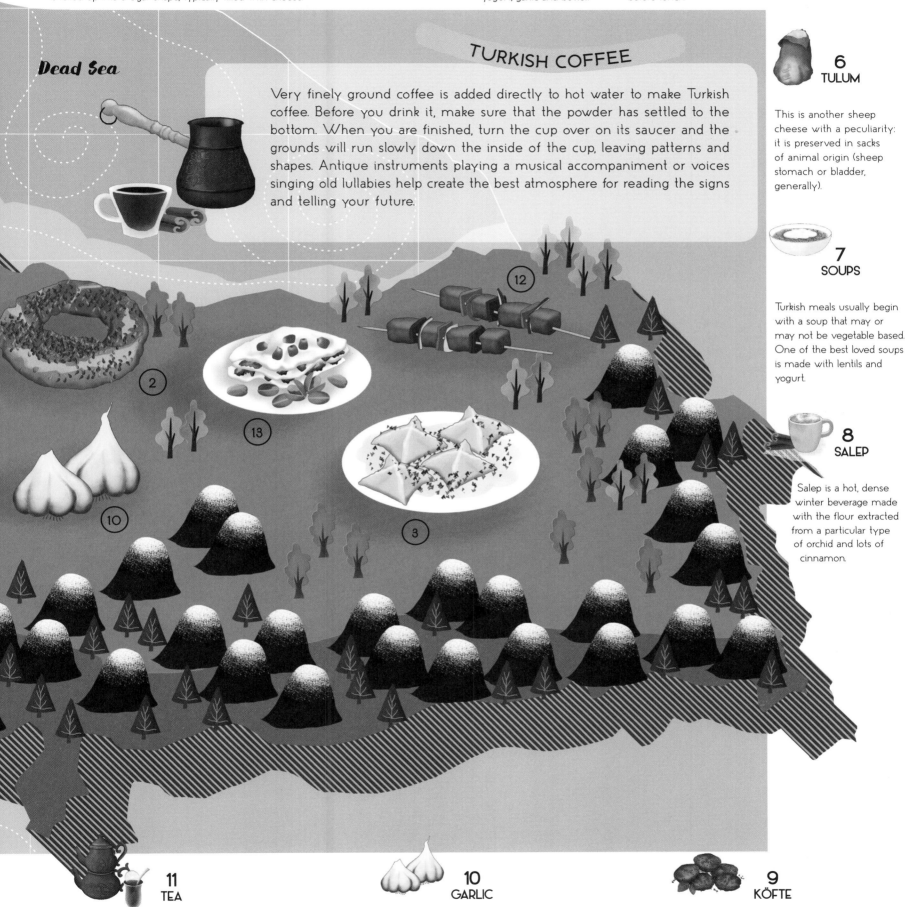

11
TEA

Every country has its own way to make tea. Turkish tea is made in a special teapot with two stacked kettles. When the tea is poured, the more concentrated tea in the upper kettle mixes with the weaker tea from the lower one to make a thoroughly balanced drink. Lavish amounts of tea are consumed throughout the day.

10
GARLIC

It is likely that the use and possibly the abuse of garlic in Turkish cuisine stems from a series of old popular beliefs. Garlic hung in the doorway was supposed to ward off misfortune and the garlic wreaths that young men hung around their necks were said to bring good luck.

9
KÖFTE

These typical little balls are easy to find just about anywhere. The classic version is made with meat, but the vegetarian version is also popular. Both are aromatized with cumin, oregano and mint. Yogurt and vegetable sauces are served on the side.

RUSSIA

The opulent and extravagant tsarist cuisine was created by the French chefs who lived and worked in the Tsar's court and is the best known Russian cuisine in the world. But traditional Russian cuisine is quite the opposite: poor and tied to products of a vast but difficult territory, it offers a small variety of dishes that are adapted according to the season and the region. Russia is geographically divided into three zones: the north, where the climate is cold; the central region, with freezing winters and temperate summers; the south, where the rainy areas meet the steppes and where most of the grain and tubers that feed the country are grown. Throughout the country, the most common dishes belong to two main categories: soups and fish, both freshwater and from the sea. Pastries are also common and are usually eaten with tea, which is served with pleasure at all hours of the day.

Kara Sea

Barents Sea

Ice-cream

RUSSIAN SALAD

This is not the simple potato salad of the same name that Europeans find in their supermarkets. The original was created by a French cook that worked in a restaurant in Moscow and had medallions of lobster, cubes of truffle, cow's tongue and a multitude of vegetables in a classic mayonnaise sauce. Nowadays, it is served on special occasions, sometimes with chicken breast added, or as an appetizer.

11 KASHA

An old adage says that Russian cuisine is Shchi and Kasha—soup and porridge. Russians have a great variety of grains at their disposal, but they prevalently soak them and cook them in milk and eat them in dishes resembling Italian polenta or English porridge.
   The most common breakfast porridge is made with buckwheat.

12 KOMPOT

The woods in the countryside are rich with berries that the Russians gather to make cold, non-alcoholic, sweet beverages that they serve in the summer.

13 PELMENI

Dried pasta is not common here, but there are many types of stuffed fresh pasta, like these dumplings with meat filling. They are served with sour cream, butter and often poppy seeds.

1
SMETANA

A dense and full-bodied sour cream, smetana is used as an accompaniment or as a base for an array of soups and tubers.

2
BORSCHT

Russia's most famous dish, this soup is made of meat and bright red beets and gets its sweet and sour flavor from the vinegar and sugar used to prepare it.

3
KVASS

Fermented grains are at the base of this alcoholic drink, typical of the Ukraine. It is also used to prepare a cold soup with mixed meats, parsley, cucumbers and the ever present smetana.

4
DILL

Dill is widely used in Russian cuisine. The seeds come from a plant with beautiful yellow flowers and are added to both fish and meat dishes to make them more flavorful and easier to digest.

5
BREAD

You'll always find bread (and potatoes) on a Russian table. It might be made of wheat (kalach) or rye (borodinsky) or be flat like a tortilla (lavash).

6
PRYANIK

This sweet, delicious dessert, bread and honey, is not actually bread at all. It is a giant cookie made with nuts and spices, decorated with a glaze and served with tea.

7
CAVIAR

You can enjoy caviar on a canapé or as a garnish in a bowl of soup. These black eggs come from the sturgeon fish that is very common in these regions. In order to preserve them, the eggs are salted when they are collected.

8
BEEF STROGANOFF

Filet of beef is cut into thin strips and cooked in sour cream with onions and mushrooms. There are two legends surrounding the name of this dish. One narrates that it was first prepared by Count Pavel Stroganoff's French chef who added the sour cream to the beef to give it more flavor. The other says that Stroganoff was the name of the doctor who used a meat based diet to cure a case of food poisoning that the tsarina got from anchovies.

9
COULIBIAC

Brioche dough is used to make this savory torte. It is a very practical dish since it is easy to transport and can be filled with almost anything, making it a rich all-in-one dish. The version with salmon also has onions, rice, mushrooms and eggs.

10
MEDOVIK

This rich, opulent Russian cake originated with the tsarist cuisine and was truly fit for the table of an emperor. Sponge cake is thinly sliced and filled with butter cream, cream, and honey.

Laptev Sea

Bering Sea

Pacific Ocean

BLINIS

Blinis are small fritters that are served with sour cream and caviar or salmon. To make them, separate the yolks from the whites of 3 eggs. Mix the yolks with 150 ml (2/3 cup) of heavy cream and 250 g (2 cups) of flour. Add a bit of yeast, 150 g (1 cup and 1 tbsp) of buckwheat flour, 100 ml (1/2 cup) of milk, 120 g (1/2 cup) of melted butter and a pinch of salt. Beat the egg whites till they're stiff and add them to the batter. Allow the batter to rest for 20 minutes then cook it in small spoonfuls that will make fritters of about 10 cm (4 in) in diameter.

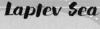

1
SHAWARMA

Thinly sliced meat, usually ovine, is skewered onto a spit and placed upright over the heat. The uppermost layer is mutton fat that melts and drips down over the rest while it is cooking. This keeps the meat both moist and crispy. The meat is served in pita bread with sauces and vegetables.

2
FALAFEL

Chickpeas are left to soak overnight then blended with lots of garlic and sesame paste and fried to make this typical dish, customarily eaten with a salad and some pita bread.

3
TABBOULEH

Generally served as a cold salad, this dish is made with couscous and huge amounts of parsley, mint, garlic, and lemon.

KECHEK EL FOUQARA

This product is also known as "poor man's cheese" since no milk is used to make it. It originated on Lebanon's southern coast near the city of Tyre and the original ancient recipe called for wheat fermented in water and sea salt. The recipe has changed over the years in several regions and some of the many variants now include the use of yogurt or goat's milk. The basic recipe still uses bulgur left to ferment for a couple of weeks that is then reduced to a paste, aromatized with spices and made into little rounds of grain "cheese".

Dried sardines and oily fish

Mediterranean Sea

7
FREEKEH

It is a grain food made from green durum wheat. It is used to prepare first course dishes. Historically harvested in the region of Jabal Amel, it is left to dry for 24 hours, then toasted on hot stones that give it its typical smoky flavor.

8
ZA'ATAR

This mix of toasted sesame seeds, dried herbs and spices is conventionally used to make bread, to flavor dipping oil for pizza or pita bread and to spice up meat or fish marinades.

38

4
KIBBEH

These fried balls of meat and bulgur wheat are Lebanon's national dish. Bulgur is cracked wheat that is steamed, dried and then finely ground. You can add a number of ingredients to these meatballs: mint, pine nuts, basil, hazelnuts, tahini sauce and any type of spice you have on hand.

5
SEMOLINA AND SAFFRON CAKE

Lebanese sweets are complicated and not easy to make at home. One exception is this saffron scented cake made with semolina flour and then soaked in syrup to keep it sweet and moist. It is often served to children as an afterschool snack.

6
STUFFED VEGETABLES

The plains of Lebanon are extremely fertile. The vegetables that grow in abundance are often prepared with a filling and served as an all-in-one dish. The filling, usually made with meat and rice and plenty of the spices that are typical of Middle Eastern culture, is used to stuff zucchini, squash, and eggplant that are then baked and served with a yogurt and tahini based sauce.

LEBANON

Lebanese cuisine is a delightful mix of Turkish and Arabic flavors with a touch of French influence—spicy, fresh and refined. It is the perfect fusion of Mediterranean foods and is undoubtedly one of the most enticing cuisines in the world. The nation's rich and florid agriculture provides cooks with all the fresh, high quality ingredients they need to prepare the courses of a typical meal—an appetizer, a main dish with meat or fish, a salad, and dessert.

Some favorite appetizers are spinach pie, cheese and pizza. They are generally served with sauces and creamy legume dishes. Tabbouleh and fattoush are salads you can find all over the country, but the national dish is kibbeh, which is made with finely ground lamb and bulgur wheat and served raw, fried or baked. Both alcoholic beverages, such as arak, and non-alcoholic beverages, such as jellab and ayran, are typical, but the most commonly consumed beverage is coffee. The Lebanese drink it at all hours of the day.

HUMMUS

This delicious cream of chickpeas is simple to make. Blend cooked chickpeas with a few spoons of water, tahini sauce, lemon juice, a clove of garlic, cumin, and paprika. Serve your hummus with bread or grilled vegetables. You can make endless versions of this cream by adding cooked vegetables such as zucchini, peppers or squash to the basic recipe.

9
LABNA

This soft creamy cheese is derived from yogurt culture or fermented milk. It is simple to make at home. All you have to do is put some yogurt into a gauze pouch and let it drain all night. It is used to prepare a lot of dishes both sweet and savory.

10
SUMAC

Sumac was originally used to dye fabrics a rosy red color. Nowadays, it is dried and used to give color and aroma to a myriad of dishes, particularly salads and cheeses.

11
FATTOUSH

A salad made with flat bread and an array of vegetables dressed with lemon and tahini sauce, this is one of Lebanon's most common dishes.

12
MA'AMOUL

These typical shortbread cookies filled with dates, pistachios and walnuts are as delicate as they are energizing. Using wooden molds to prepare them makes it possible to fill them without ruining their shape. Muslims eat ma'amoul in the evenings during Ramadan, Christians make them for Easter and the Jewish make them for the holidays of Purim and Tu BiShvat.

1
AMBA

This mango sauce is used on sandwiches made with vegetables and eggs or filled with shawarma—a dish made with mutton, turkey or chicken covered with sheep fat.

2
SABICH

Fried eggplant nestled in pita bread full of sauce and lettuce may not be the most digestible dish in the world, but it certainly is one you ought to try!

3
BUREKAS

These typically Middle Eastern phyllo pastries are filled with meat or mashed vegetables. They are always very spicy.

4
KABEES

It is impossible to walk around a market in Israel without finding big basins full of kabees. These brightly colored, phosphorescent pickled vegetables served with meat or salad are a national favorite.

5
MEJADRA

Basmati rice, lentils, spices and crispy onion are the basis for this dish also known as Esau's soup, with reference to its Jewish origins. Similar versions are common throughout the Middle East.

ISRAEL

The fact that Israeli cuisine comes from blend of cultures makes it difficult to define and classify. Here, you will find Middle Eastern dishes on the same table with Jewish food. Over the centuries, emigrant Jews from all over the world have enriched the country's culinary customs and instilled a multicultural identity in a cuisine whose dishes are common in nearly every corner of the Earth. Israelis use drip irrigation to cultivate the abundance of vegetables that are a constant in their dishes. It has been said that they could make the sand bloom in the desert!

LATKES

These little potato fritters are perfect with hummus and muhamarra, but they are also delicious by themselves. Even though they are traditionally prepared for Hanukkah, the Festival of Lights, you can surprise your friends and family with them any time of the year. These are the ingredients: 4 potatoes, 1 egg, 1 tablespoon of flour and 1 onion. Slice the onion and grate the potatoes and let them dry for a minute or two before mixing them with the flour and egg. Spoon the dough into hot oil, fry them till they are golden and serve them hot.

6
JERUSALEM KUGEL

Countless versions of this casserole exist, both savory (frequently made with carrots and potatoes) and sweet. Jerusalem Kugel is a sweet version—slathered in caramel.

7
SHAKSHOUKA

Jewish Tunisians brought this dish to Israel. It is made with onion, garlic, tomatoes, peppers and eggs and seasoned with black pepper and other spices. The eggs are fried and added to a vegetable sauce—finger-licking perfect with pita bread.

8
JERUSALEM COUSCOUS

In Palestine, couscous is made from whole wheat semolina that has bigger grains than the ones in North Africa. In Arabic it is called "maftoul", which indicates the circular stirring movement you will need to make a perfect pot of couscous.

9
HAMANTASCHEN

The French call these triangular jam—filled cookies "oreilles d'Aman", Haman's ears. They are typically prepared to celebrate Purim, the Jewish holiday that follows a one-day fast.

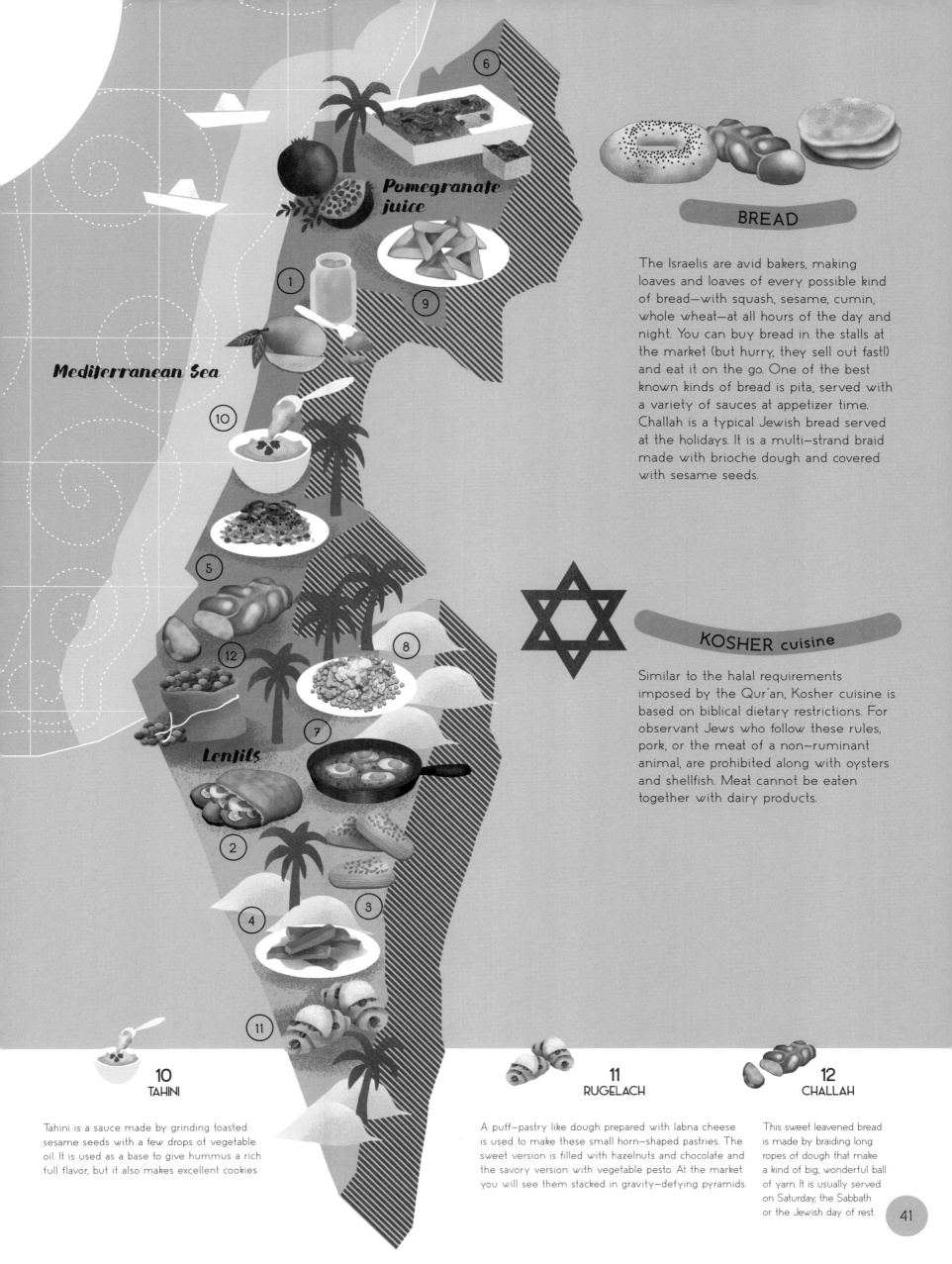

Pomegranate juice

Mediterranean Sea

Lentils

BREAD

The Israelis are avid bakers, making loaves and loaves of every possible kind of bread—with squash, sesame, cumin, whole wheat—at all hours of the day and night. You can buy bread in the stalls at the market (but hurry, they sell out fast!) and eat it on the go. One of the best known kinds of bread is pita, served with a variety of sauces at appetizer time. Challah is a typical Jewish bread served at the holidays. It is a multi-strand braid made with brioche dough and covered with sesame seeds.

KOSHER cuisine

Similar to the halal requirements imposed by the Qur'an, Kosher cuisine is based on biblical dietary restrictions. For observant Jews who follow these rules, pork, or the meat of a non-ruminant animal, are prohibited along with oysters and shellfish. Meat cannot be eaten together with dairy products.

10 TAHINI

Tahini is a sauce made by grinding toasted sesame seeds with a few drops of vegetable oil. It is used as a base to give hummus a rich full flavor, but it also makes excellent cookies.

11 RUGELACH

A puff-pastry like dough prepared with labna cheese is used to make these small horn-shaped pastries. The sweet version is filled with hazelnuts and chocolate and the savory version with vegetable pesto. At the market you will see them stacked in gravity-defying pyramids.

12 CHALLAH

This sweet leavened bread is made by braiding long ropes of dough that make a kind of big, wonderful ball of yarn. It is usually served on Saturday, the Sabbath or the Jewish day of rest.

1
PURI

Puri pastries are made with chickpea flour and fried in abundant oil until they become crispy and light. They are served as an accompaniment to the main courses.

2
PAKORA

Pakora are vegetable fritters dipped in a batter made of chickpea flour and water. They can be found in stands along the road as street food.

3
GHEE

Cooks in India often use a butter from which the water has been removed, leaving only the fat. This allows it to resist at the much higher temperatures that develop in the direct heat ovens.

4
KULFI

Indians like ice cream too, but they use just milk to make it. Big pans of milk are left to condense over a fire for up to 4 hours and are then flavored with hazelnut or pistachio paste before being frozen in molds.

TANDOOR

Tandoor cooking, typical in the Punjab region, uses a very special clay oven that is buried in the ground and filled with charcoal (or, in the poorer regions, cow dung). The mouth of the oven is level with the ground and is used to introduce the food to be cooked. Roti bread is cooked by pressing it to the oven walls and is done when it falls off.

11
BIRYANI

Biryani is the essence of all Indian dishes. Made with boiled basmati rice and flavored with turmeric and saffron, it is enriched with ingredients that are all cooked and added separately: meat (particularly chicken), vegetables or fish, together with dried fruit and nuts. It is flavored with ginger, pepper, chili pepper, coriander, cumin and any other available spice.

42

5
LASSI

This yogurt—based drink is flavored with spices and fruit. It is usually drunk in small sips after a meal as a digestive and is loved by both children and adults.

6
JALEBI

Typical of all Asian countries, this dessert is made of a chickpea and corn flour batter that it is left to rise with yogurt for an entire night. It is then shaped into spirals, fried and dipped in honey.

7
CHUTNEY

Chutney can be described as a sweet and sour jam made with fruit and vegetables mixed together to serve with meat and boiled fish.

8
CURRY

In India this mix of spices is actually called masala and is a mustard yellow—colored powder that should be pan—toasted before using it. The stews prepared with this spice are also called curries.

9
GULAB JAMUN

These small fritters are made with semolina and powdered milk. The spongy little balls are dipped in a syrup made of water, sugar and orange blossoms that make them especially aromatic.

10
CHAI TEA

This very strong black tea is aromatized with cinnamon and cardamom and served with hot milk and sugar and cardamom sweets.

INDIA

Indian cuisine varies greatly from region to region, but Punjab cuisine is the one that has become famous throughout the world. The one characteristic common to all of the regions is the abundant use of milk, cheeses, and spices that have spread from here to the rest of the world thanks to the merchants who traveled these routes and considered the spices a tradable commodity more valuable than gold. In the northern regions the use of meat is also common, while in the sub—continent (India is so big that it is often referred to this way) most dishes are mainly meatless with a rich variety of vegetables.

Indian Ocean

CHICKEN CURRY

This very simple dish is spiced up with curry powder and coconut milk. Prepare it and serve it with simple white rice. Have your butcher clean a chicken breast for you. Cut it into small pieces. Sauté it in a bit of butter with a finely chopped onion. Add a good sized spoon of curry powder, finely chopped almonds and a few ladles full of broth. Let the chicken cook through, then add the coconut milk and cook for a few minutes more. Serve with white rice, preferably cooked pilaf style.

12
TURMERIC

This spice, called Indian gold for its golden color, is very rich in anti—oxidants. It is used in abundance in masala—based dishes.

13
THALI

Thali is the most famous multi—course dish named after the tray used to serve it. The plate is divided into sections so that the various courses of the meal remain separate.

14
CHAPATI

Cheese or garlic are sometimes used to fill this unleavened bread, which is then cooked on the tawa— a red—hot grill pan. It is served with vegetables or meat fresh off of the fire.

15
TAMARIND

This plant is also known as the Indian date. It is a very common spice used to prepare sambhar, one of India's most widely known dishes made with lentils and vegetables. The fruit is also eaten after simple drying, especially in the eastern most parts of the country.

1
TOFU AND SOY

Soy has been grown in China for more than 5,000 years. Its beans are used in a large variety of preparations, ranging from the condiments made with fermented beans to tofu, a cheese–like ingredient made with soy milk rennet and used as protein in many Chinese dishes.

2
BAOZI

Also known as bao, these buns are filled with meat or vegetables and steamed. They are usually eaten as an accompaniment to the main course.

3
STEAM COOKING

One of the most common ways to cook in China, this method uses bamboo baskets stacked one on top of the other and then placed on top of a wok full of boiling water.

4
SPRING ROLLS

A mix of vegetables that always includes leeks and cabbage are rolled up in rice paper wrappers and fried.

5
SILKIE CHICKEN

The silkie chicken's characteristically dark meat is used to make a soup that is considered an exquisitely elegant dish.

CHINA

Chinese cuisine is one of the oldest in the world. Its roots can be found in the ancient dictates of Chinese medicine that associate foods with two opposite but complementary energies, Yin and Yang. In order to be balanced, dishes have to include foods from both categories.

It is not surprising that a multitude of variants on the country's traditional dishes have developed in a territory as vast as China. There are so many dishes that to describe them (or even simply to discover them) is practically impossible. Certainly one of the most common foods here is rice. China is the biggest producer in the world and the image of bowed heads protected by dŏuli, a typical conical Asian hat, is common during the annual rice harvest.

CANTONESE RICE

Cantonese rice is a truly rich dish. Heat 5 tablespoons of vegetable oil in a heavy skillet. Add a finely chopped spring onion, 300 g (2 cups) of boiled basmati rice and 150 g (5 oz) of spring peas. When they are heated through, add cubed ham, 3 tablespoons of soy sauce and a pinch of salt. In a bowl, beat 3 eggs and add them to the hot skillet for last, stirring constantly. Serve the rice hot and have fun eating it with your chopsticks.

9
FIVE-SPICE POWDER

This traditional mix of Chinese spices made with pepper, star anise, cinnamon, cloves and fennel seeds is used practically everywhere.

10
LOTUS

Every part of the lotus plant is edible: you can eat its buds raw and its spectacular roots, which taste a bit like beets, can be used as a vegetable in soups or grilled.

11
CENTURY EGGS

To make century eggs, or 100–year–old eggs, duck eggs are preserved in a solution of clay, salt, ash, quicklime and rice hulls for anywhere from a few weeks to a number of months. The inside of the eggs turn to a brownish–black color and even though they may not look appealing, they are considered a real delicacy by the Chinese who enjoy them on many occasions.

12
WONTON

These dumplings are made of an ultrathin wrapper filled with meat, vegetables or shrimp. They are steamed and then browned on the grill pan or fried.

13
SOY AND RICE NOODLES

The Chinese are often cited as the inventors of spaghetti. They prevalently use soy and rice to make the noodles that they serve with vegetables, meat and abundant soy sauce.

6
OYSTER SAUCE

This sauce is made by boiling oysters and adding sugar, caramel and salt to the liquid obtained. Its flavor is intense and it's usually used on meat or as a sauce for spring rolls and dumplings.

7
DRAGON EYE OR LONGAN

This fruit certainly does not look inviting but it is actually delicious and full of vitamin C. It is used in Chinese medicine to aid the memory and the heart.

8
SHARK FINS

No allegory this time around—they really are shark fins. The fins are used in an ancient recipe to make a soup that is traditionally served at banquets and feasts.

Using CHOPSTICKS

Legend has it that Daji, the concubine of the bad-tempered King Zhou of Shang saved the king's cook from persecution. He was about to serve the king a dish that was dangerously hot, so Daji used one of her jade hair pins to feed him. This happened long before the fork was invented and ever since, the Chinese have used long, thin wooden sticks to bring their food to their mouths. Food is served in small bites so no knife is necessary. In fact, knives in China are considered kitchen tools, not to be brought to the table.

China Seas

45

1
SINSEOLLO

This typical cooking vessel, also called a royal hot pot, resembles a Bundt pan with a hole in the middle used to cook special meals for banquets and important festive occasions. It is used to prepare an elaborate lasagna—like dish of the same name made with meatballs, mushrooms and vegetables.

2
INSECTS

In Korea eating insects is a perfectly normal occurrence. Silk worm cocoons are sold on the streets in paper cones, especially in the summer. Those who have tasted them say their flavor is sweetish and persistent. Roasted red ants are also common and are said to be good for heartburn.

3
MEDICINAL FOODS

Korean cuisine is full of particular animals and animal parts like snakes and deer or goat's horns that are available in neighborhood markets and are eaten for therapeutic purposes.

KOREA

Korean cuisine is among the oldest on Earth. Rice dishes are the main component and are traditionally served with meat and vegetables and a surprising number of side dishes at every meal.

Fermentation is a common method, used both to preserve vegetables and to make them light and digestible. The national dish is kimchi. It shows up in almost every meal and is actually the main ingredient in many dishes. It is the symbol of conviviality in Korean culture where gathering around the table together is an essential moment in family life.

KIMCHI

Brine fermented fresh cabbage and chili pepper are combined to make Kimchi, the most traditional Korean dish. Wash the leaves of 2 big heads of Chinese cabbage (Napa cabbage), cut them into quarters and layer them in a terrine with coarse salt. Cover them with cold water and let them sit for a night. Chop 3 spring onions, 1 clove of garlic, a piece of horseradish root, 2 carrots, a piece of ginger, 50 g (3 tbsp and 1 tsp) of salt and 100 gr (3.5 oz) of chili pepper and add the mixture to the drained cabbage. Transfer the cabbage to sterilized jars, cover it with the brine and let it ferment for 3 to 6 days before eating it.

4
BUNGEOPPANG

These fish shaped wafers filled with red bean jam are also common in Japan. They are often sold as street food.

5
HOTTEOK

Made with a dough of flour, water, yeast and sugar, these Korean pancakes usually have a delectable filling of honey, peanuts and cinnamon.

6
DALGONA

Designs are imprinted on these beautiful lollipops made of caramel and baking soda. Anyone who is able to eat one without ruining the design gets to have another one.

7
KOREAN HOT DOGS

While it is certainly not the oldest dish, these hot dogs dipped in batter, covered in potato chips and fried are a decidedly tasty treat to eat on the road.

8
ODENG

You can find these fragrant fish skewers boiled in a spicy broth in the markets of South Korea.

9
TTEOKBOKKI

Chili pepper spices up these simple stir—fried rice cakes. They are cooked in the wok and then seasoned with a super—hot sauce.

HANSIK

A Korean meal is generally very simple: an all—in—one dish with steamed rice is served with a broth base soup made with meat, fish and vegetables. Meals are served on a typical table and a series of very specific rules are strictly observed. Every table has to have 5 colors and an odd number of plates. The soup bowls have to be to the right of the rice bowls and only when the oldest diner (who is also generally the one to pay the bill) starts eating, can the other diners pick up their chopsticks and eat too.

Yellow Sea

Sea of Japan

10
PERILLA LEAVES

Perilla leaves taste like a mix between basil and mint and are frequently used to aromatize Korean soups and stews.

11
LIVE MOLLUSKS

It is an extreme experience because even after it has been cut, the mollusk keeps moving. Only the brave will try the most popular dishes in this category: sea snails and small octopuses.

12
DOENJANG

This soft pasty condiment is made with fermented beans and is mixed with sesame oil and vinegar to dress rice and vegetables.

47

1
SUSHI AND SASHIMI

Sushi is a composition of glutinous rice (full of starch so very sticky when it is cooked). It is made with vinegar and sweet sake or mirin and served with either raw or cooked fish, eggs and seaweed. Sashimi, which is simply raw fish, gets its name from its particular cut.

2
TAMAGOYAKI

Mirin and sugar are used to make this omelet that is cooked in a special square skillet (makiyakinabe) and then rolled up to resemble a big snake.

3
ADZUKI BEAN PASTE (ANKO)

For Japanese children, this is the equivalent of a westerner's chocolate spread. A unique delight, it is used on dorayaki, typical little fritters similar to pancakes.

4
GYOZA

These are the famous steamed or grilled dumplings we all know. They can be stuffed with a myriad of fillings and then pinched closed without adding egg whites or water.

5
TAIYAKI

This fish-shaped waffle-like dessert, created in Tokyo in 1909, can be sweet, filled with anko or chocolate, or savory, filled with cheese or the same ingredients used for gyoza stuffing.

JAPAN

One of the most remarkable things about Japanese food is that it was created to be eaten first with your eyes and then with your mouth. Dishes go beyond being delicious—everything is meticulously prepared and presented as well. Geometry, symmetry and a harmony of colors and shapes are mandatory elements in a Japanese meal. All dishes are brought to the table at the same time so that each diner can eat them in the order that pleases him or her. Food is eaten with chopsticks—only the cooks in the kitchen can use the world famous battery of Japanese knives and other cutting tools. The flavors of foods are also meticulously studied in order to preserve the purest tastes possible. In fact, the tendency is toward raw ingredients, served separately with sauces rigorously on the side.

ONIGIRI

Bentō, the equivalent of our home-packed lunch box, is a veritable institution. Great attention is given to every detail of these meals that are often true works of art. Onigiri, the star of the bento show, are rice balls with a variety of fillings. They are usually triangular but may also be made in many other, sometimes strange, shapes.

To make them, heat some vinegar with a spoonful of sugar and add it to boiled sushi rice. While it is cooling, grill a piece of salmon, add salt and soy sauce and break it up with a fork. In the palm of your hand, place a bit of rice, add the salmon, roll the mix first into a ball and then make it into a triangle. Garnish it with a ribbon of nori seaweed and put it in your bentō.

7
GOMASHIO

It is a mix of sea salt and sesame seeds and sometimes seaweed. It is used as a condiment for rice or onigiri.

8
WASABI

Wasabi is the official accompaniment for sushi and sashimi. It is a paste made with a ground, green radish that belongs to the same family as horseradish and that grows in the colder parts of the country. It is spicy and pungent and must be used with caution.

9
RAMEN

This typical dish made with wheat flour noodles served in broth with pork or eggs or fish and any number of vegetables has become very trendy.

10
KOBE BEEF

It is one of the most expensive and prestigious kinds of meat in the world. The cows are massaged and fed only delicacies to produce a tender meat with perfectly distributed fat stores.

11
UDON

These thick noodles are normally made with durum wheat and served in broth. You will also find them served with vegetables, soy, meat and fish to satisfy western tastes.

48

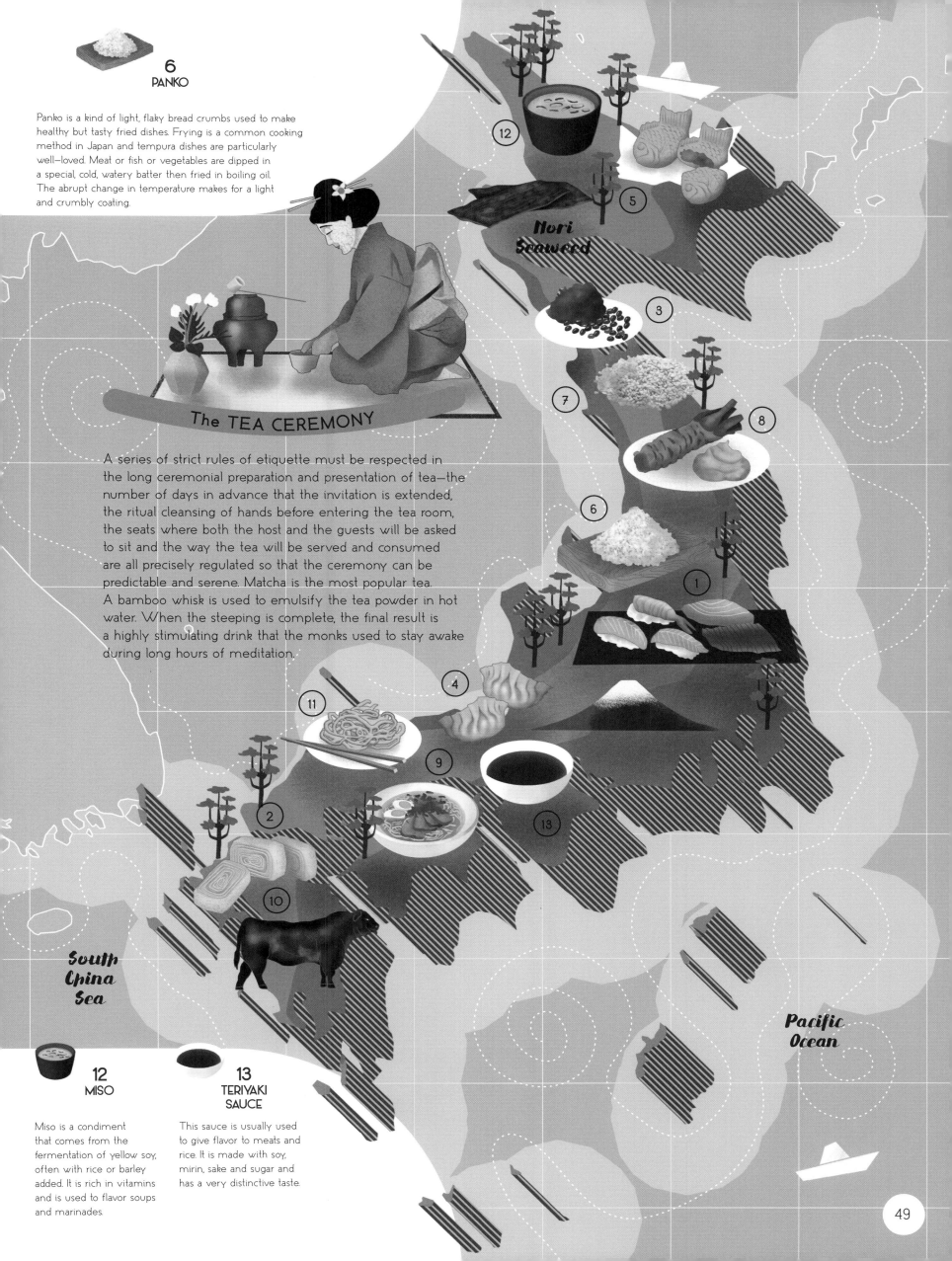

6
PANKO

Panko is a kind of light, flaky bread crumbs used to make healthy but tasty fried dishes. Frying is a common cooking method in Japan and tempura dishes are particularly well-loved. Meat or fish or vegetables are dipped in a special, cold, watery batter then fried in boiling oil. The abrupt change in temperature makes for a light and crumbly coating.

The TEA CEREMONY

A series of strict rules of etiquette must be respected in the long ceremonial preparation and presentation of tea—the number of days in advance that the invitation is extended, the ritual cleansing of hands before entering the tea room, the seats where both the host and the guests will be asked to sit and the way the tea will be served and consumed are all precisely regulated so that the ceremony can be predictable and serene. Matcha is the most popular tea. A bamboo whisk is used to emulsify the tea powder in hot water. When the steeping is complete, the final result is a highly stimulating drink that the monks used to stay awake during long hours of meditation.

Nori Seaweed

South China Sea

Pacific Ocean

12
MISO

Miso is a condiment that comes from the fermentation of yellow soy, often with rice or barley added. It is rich in vitamins and is used to flavor soups and marinades.

13
TERIYAKI SAUCE

This sauce is usually used to give flavor to meats and rice. It is made with soy, mirin, sake and sugar and has a very distinctive taste.

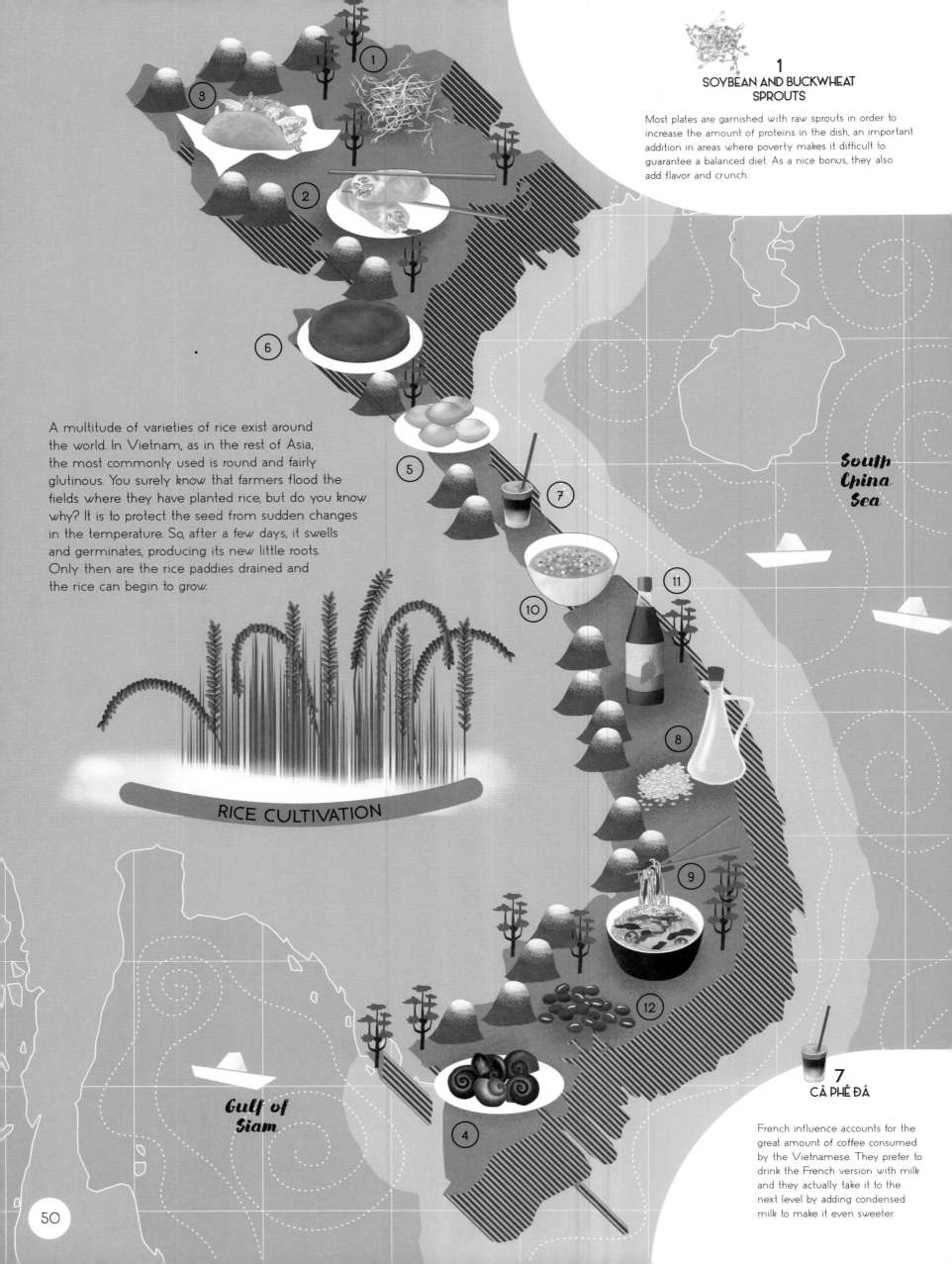

1
SOYBEAN AND BUCKWHEAT SPROUTS

Most plates are garnished with raw sprouts in order to increase the amount of proteins in the dish, an important addition in areas where poverty makes it difficult to guarantee a balanced diet. As a nice bonus, they also add flavor and crunch.

South China Sea

A multitude of varieties of rice exist around the world. In Vietnam, as in the rest of Asia, the most commonly used is round and fairly glutinous. You surely know that farmers flood the fields where they have planted rice, but do you know why? It is to protect the seed from sudden changes in the temperature. So, after a few days, it swells and germinates, producing its new little roots. Only then are the rice paddies drained and the rice can begin to grow.

RICE CULTIVATION

Gulf of Siam

7
CÀ PHÊ ĐÁ

French influence accounts for the great amount of coffee consumed by the Vietnamese. They prefer to drink the French version with milk and they actually take it to the next level by adding condensed milk to make it even sweeter.

2
SPRING ROLLS

Spring rolls are characteristic of Vietnamese cuisine: many dishes are rolled in a rice wafer and eaten raw or fried. Fillings are usually made with ground meat, fish, simple vegetables or rice noodles.

3
BÁNH KHOÁI

Shrimp, vegetables and spices fill this rice flour crepe. Rolled in a rice wrapper and fried, it is then served with yellow beans.

4
SNAILS

Snails are an absolute delicacy in Vietnam. They can be eaten stewed or rolled up in the ever present wraps.

5
BÁNH BÒ

This little rice cake is spongy and soft and sometimes has a slight aftertaste of coconut milk. It is often soaked in syrup to make it even sweeter.

6
BEAN CAKE

This is a common cake made with tapioca starch, rice flour, mung beans, taro, coconut milk and sugar. Mixed together, they have a delicious but very particular flavor.

VIETNAM

Vietnamese culinary traditions are among the oldest in Asia. Someone counted the country's existing traditional dishes and apparently there are nearly 500. The importance that the Vietnamese give to their food is demonstrated by an old local adage that says "one should learn to eat before learning to talk". After the war, French influence was added to the Asiatic base of this cuisine making the food even more refined and particular. Here as in other Asian countries, rice is the most important dietary staple. The rest of the food is based on a harmony of colors, tastes and aromas, with very little meat since it is prohibited by Buddhism, which is one of the most widely practiced religions in this country.

SINH TỒ BO

The recipe for Sinh Tồ Bo, one of Vietnam's best loved desserts, is simple and easy to follow. To make this smoothie, blend an avocado with a couple of tablespoons of sweetened, condensed milk and add a few mint leaves to give it a hint of freshness.

8
SESAME OIL

The seeds of the sesame plant are ground to produce this intensely and persistently flavored oil. A few drops are enough to give a dish character. It is one of the few fats used in this otherwise very dietetic cuisine.

9
PHỞ

This soup is considered a national dish. Meat broth is served with noodles and little strips of meat and soy sprouts. Lime, lemongrass and basil give it a flavor that's both fresh and energizing.

10
NƯỚC CHẤM

This shrimp paste is obtained by grinding whole crustaceans and is used as a flavor enhancer in just about every savory dish.

11
FERMENTED FISH SAUCE

Fish sauce is an essential ingredient in Vietnamese cuisine. Raw fish, primarily anchovies and shellfish, is left to ferment in wooden crates with salt and other seasonings. When it has fermented, the mix is slowly pressed to extract the liquid. Oddly, this sauce does not taste like fish; the fermentation gives it a flavor similar to aged cheese.

12
MUNG BEANS

These are green soy beans that are husked and ground into powder. Surprisingly, they are mostly used to make ice cream and popsicles.

1
DURIAN

It is considered the king of fruit in Thailand because of its sweet taste. Unfortunately, its smell is nauseating. It is strictly forbidden to take it into a store or eat it in a closed environment. It is just too stinky. In southeastern Thailand no fruit is better loved. When it is sold fresh, its sweet pulp is soft and creamy, but you can also buy it in cans or dried.

2
BANANA ROTI

This roti, a flat bread, is served with caramelized bananas and condensed milk.

3
CURRY

Contrary to Indian curry, Thai curry is generally used in a paste form and can be red or green. Red curry paste is made with dried chili peppers mixed with other spices and is quite hot. Green curry paste gets its hint of lemon from lemongrass and, since it is made with green peppers, it is slightly less hot.

4
KAFFIR LIME

The juice of this citrus fruit, also called combava, is so acidic that it must be eaten cooked, never raw. Its grated peel is aromatic and is used to flavor fish dishes.

THAILAND

Thai food is distinguished from other oriental cuisines by the delicate balance between 5 fundamental flavors—sweet, sour, salty, bitter, and umami—that are always present and always equilibrated. In the western world, umami is a taste few people know, but in Asia it is at the heart of many dishes. It comes from the taste of sodium glutamate contained in condiments such as bouillon or soy sauce or in cheese or meat. It could be translated as "savory". Herbs, spices and rice are part of almost every recipe even if their use varies from region to region and may be influenced by neighboring countries.

COCONUT MILK

Coconut milk is often used to flavor curry dishes, but it also makes a great smoothie if you blend it with fresh fruit. Making coconut milk is simple: break open a coconut, eliminate the water and the shell and keep the pulp. Weigh the pulp and slightly heat the double of that weight in water. Add the water to the pulp, blend it together then strain it in a fine mesh colander. The white liquid that you get is coconut milk!

Indian Ocean

8
KAENG TAI PLA

This soup, made with fish entrails and grilled, fermented fish, is typical of southern Thailand.

9
HOI TOD

This crispy "flower" of flour and eggs is halfway between a pancake and an omelet. It is filled with mussels, sprouts, soy sauce, vinegar and a thousand other seasonings.

10
INSECTS

Here as in other parts of the world, insects are eaten as snacks. Red palm weevils, for instance are sweet and sour and are used to enrich salads. Street kiosks sell wasps nests rolled in banana leaves and grilled. Larvae are a fried delicacy while giant water bugs are boiled or fried then salted or crushed and added to the curry sauce used to make nam phrik, a genuinely traditional Thai dish.

11
BOAT NOODLES

These rice noodles are served in dense soups made with meat and pig's blood. Their name derives from the fact that they were originally served aboard the boats that cross the canals of Bangkok.

12
ISAAN SAUSAGE

Pork is commonly used in Thai cooking and is usually barbecued or stewed. This sausage looks like a pearl necklace. It is made with fermented rice and meat, which gives it its sweet and sour flavor.

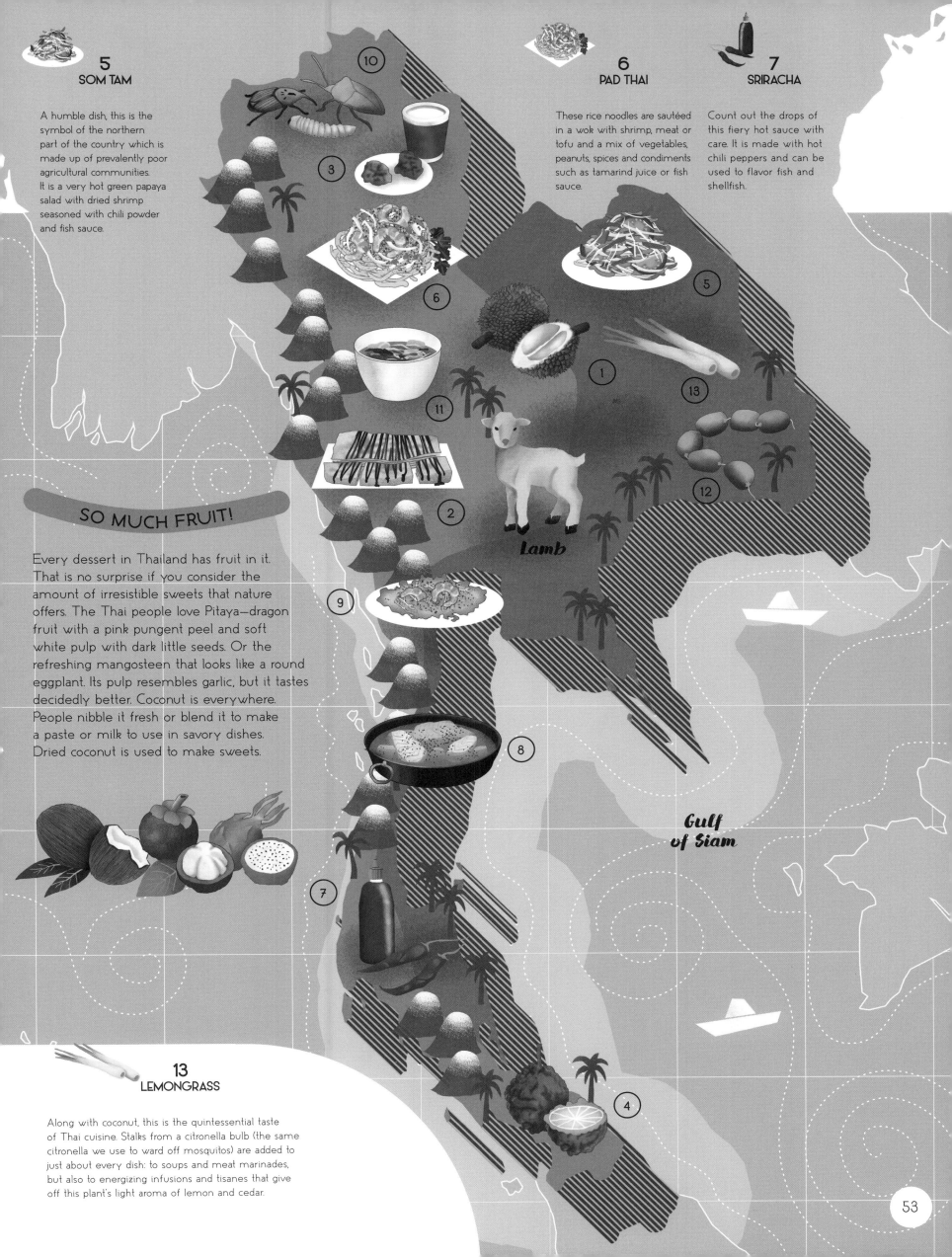

5
SOM TAM

A humble dish, this is the symbol of the northern part of the country which is made up of prevalently poor agricultural communities. It is a very hot green papaya salad with dried shrimp seasoned with chili powder and fish sauce.

6
PAD THAI

These rice noodles are sautéed in a wok with shrimp, meat or tofu and a mix of vegetables, peanuts, spices and condiments such as tamarind juice or fish sauce.

7
SRIRACHA

Count out the drops of this fiery hot sauce with care. It is made with hot chili peppers and can be used to flavor fish and shellfish.

Lamb

SO MUCH FRUIT!

Every dessert in Thailand has fruit in it. That is no surprise if you consider the amount of irresistible sweets that nature offers. The Thai people love Pitaya—dragon fruit with a pink pungent peel and soft white pulp with dark little seeds. Or the refreshing mangosteen that looks like a round eggplant. Its pulp resembles garlic, but it tastes decidedly better. Coconut is everywhere. People nibble it fresh or blend it to make a paste or milk to use in savory dishes. Dried coconut is used to make sweets.

Gulf of Siam

13
LEMONGRASS

Along with coconut, this is the quintessential taste of Thai cuisine. Stalks from a citronella bulb (the same citronella we use to ward off mosquitos) are added to just about every dish: to soups and meat marinades, but also to energizing infusions and tisanes that give off this plant's light aroma of lemon and cedar.

1	2	3	4	5	6
TEA	**SPICES**	**PALM SUGAR AND SWEET SOY SAUCE**	**SATAY**	**RICE**	**ROAST PIGLET**

1 TEA

The islands of Java and Sumatra give us what the West considers some of the most precious teas in the world. Yet here the preferred beverage after a meal is coffee.

2 SPICES

The Maluku Islands are also called the Spice Islands because many of the flavorings used around the world come from here, including cloves, nutmeg and Szechuan pepper.

3 PALM SUGAR AND SWEET SOY SAUCE

Palm sugar and sweet soy sauce are used especially in the areas of Java and are part of a sweet and sour cuisine similar to that of Thailand.

4 SATAY

Satay is a special marinade made with peanut butter, soy sauce and lime to be used on meat or fish skewers.

5 RICE

The local rice has long, fine grains and a delicate flavor. Rice is cooked in coconut milk to make this—the most common side dish to every course—even more aromatic.

6 ROAST PIGLET

This dish, which is typical of the Bali area, is roasted, flavored with coconut, garlic, chili pepper and blood pudding and served with an endless selection of sauces and vegetables.

INDONESIA

Indonesia is a country made up of 18,000 islands and islets of which 6,000 are inhabited. A mosaic of 300 different languages are spoken here. Obviously, it is difficult to imagine that there could be a common cuisine; simply getting around to tasting each and every dish seems pretty improbable too.

As usual, the spices are the star of the show and food is prevalently cooked in 5 ways: fried, grilled, steamed, boiled and stir-fried—the typical method for cooking omelets and sautéed dishes. Generally speaking, Indonesian food is simple. Dishes are cooked with great regard for their ingredients, which are almost always local. Portions are always generous and the various components of each recipe are served separately in a lot of little bowls.

SHRIMP SATAY

This is a very simple recipe: clean the shrimp and stick them on a skewer. Mix a few spoons of peanut butter with one spoonful of honey, some soy sauce and as much water as you need to make the sauce fluid. Coat the skewered shrimp with the sauce and cook them on the grill. Serve with white rice and fresh vegetables.

Java Sea

54

7
LUMPIA

Lumpia is a spring roll made with a sheet of rice pasta filled with sprouts, vegetables, palm hearts, pieces of chicken and beets. It is eaten fresh or fried.

8
NASI GORENG

This is a rice dish served with small portions of meat, vegetables or fish and an egg in the center. It is usually prepared in the market place and is served on a banana leaf.

9
ES BUAH

This well-loved sweet street food is made with fresh fruit covered in fruit gelatin and served with puffed rice and milk.

10
BUBBLE TEA

Milk, tapioca balls and fruit gelatin are added to this tea. It is one of the few indulgences toward foreign cuisine that you will find in these traditionalist islands.

11
SOTO

This meat broth prepared with pork, yearling mutton, chicken, noodles, vegetables and sometimes eggs can be found all over the country in various local versions.

12
KELEPON

Rice flour and palm sugar are used to prepare these sweet green balls that are covered in coconut flour.

Indonesia, like many other Asian countries, has particular table manners. For example, it is normal here to eat with your right hand, without a fork or a spoon. Like in Japan, knives are never on the table: they are only to be used by cooks in the kitchen. Chopsticks are rather common, but they should never be used to point at something or, worse, to pass food with, which is considered a very rude gesture. And be careful: never blow your nose at the table. It is considered a truly impolite thing to do. Better to get up and go to the bathroom to do it!

TABLE MANNERS

13
PEPES AND TUM

The ingredients in this dish are wrapped in banana leaves and then cooked on a grill (pepes) or steamed (tum). The banana leaves make the wraps soft and aromatic, but they are not to be eaten.

14
KOPI LUWAK

Why is this the most precious and expensive coffee in the world? Because the beans of this plant are a staple of the palm civet's diet. The animal has enzymes in its intestine that "clean" the beans that are then returned without the bitterness and acidity but with a hint of chocolate. All you need now is the courage to pick them out of his feces, clean them off one by one and grind them to make this precious beverage.

Pacific Ocean

NORTHERN AFRICA
page 58

CENTRAL AFRICA
page 60

SOUTHERN AFRICA
page 62

AFRICA

A CUISINE WITH A THOUSAND FLAVORS NARRATES THE LONG AND ANCIENT HISTORY OF THIS CONTINENT.

It seems nearly certain now that the very first men on earth were born here in Africa, making it the cradle of all civilization. Food here is obviously sustenance, but throughout this great continent eating is above all sharing.

Gathering around a low table laden with couscous and tajine or close to a fire where wild game is being cooked is an almost sacred ritual in which conviviality, togetherness and storytelling are almost more important than what is on your plate.

The Berbers from the desert of Northern Africa have transformed their customs that now closely resemble those of the stationary populations. The cuisine in Central and Southern Africa is often described as rainbow cuisine due to the varying influence of diverse cultures and populations, ranging from the indigenous Africans to the Europeans and Asians.

1
TAJINE

This characteristic pot uses steam to make stews of the same name with legumes and vegetables, or meat or fish. With a raised-edge dish and a conical lid, the pot creates condensation that falls into the food, keeping it soft.

2
BRIK

This extremely thin pastry is used to make sweet or savory fried dumplings in a multitude of shapes—squares, triangles, cigars, and more!

3
KEBAB

The meat for this dish is roasted on a vertical spit, then sliced very thin and served in unleavened flat bread with tomatoes, onions and lettuce, and dressed with a spicy sauce made with yogurt and harissa.

Atlantic Ocean

COUSCOUS

One way to make a good couscous is to begin with durum wheat semolina, steam it and then very patiently reduce it to little granules by hand. Otherwise, you can buy it already cooked and rehydrate it in boiling water and lemon. Little pieces of squash, zucchini, onions and pepper stewed with ras el hanout, a typical mix of spices and herbs, make an excellent sauce to serve with your couscous. To make it, brown the vegetables, add some cooked chickpeas and cover with broth that should be completely reduced by the time the dish is ready. If you want to be a traditionalist, try eating the couscous and vegetables with your hands.

MOROCCAN TEA

Moroccan tea is aromatized with mint to ward off the effects of extreme heat and since it is typically consumed in the desert, it must be effective. Moroccans drink it with their meals, pouring it from a height of at least 30 cm (12 in) from the table to make it foam. Tea is also a fundamental element for the desert Tuaregs that use a precise ceremonial ritual to offer it to their guests as a sign of welcome.

4
FŪL

Egyptian fava beans are mixed with oil, salt, pepper and abundant onion to make this dish, which was a favorite of the Pharaohs!

5
HALAL

This region is prevalently Muslim, which means that the food must be halal or "permissible". Meat in particular must be butchered according to the rules written in the Quran. The animals must arrive at the slaughterhouse alive. The slaughter has to be as humane as possible and all of the blood has to be drained from the meat before it can be eaten. Similarly strict rules apply to cheese.

6
HARIRA

This soup is typical of the Moroccan desert and the Berber culture. Made with lamb, vegetables, legumes and aromatic spices. It is generally served as the evening meal during the 30 days for Ramadan so it has to be substantial.

7
KANAFEH

This sweet is made with kataifi dough—fine crunchy threads—covered with a creamy cheese with no eggs and garnished with honey and pistachios. Like all of the pastries in this region, it is very sweet but its orange blossom scent is very refreshing.

NORTHERN AFRICA

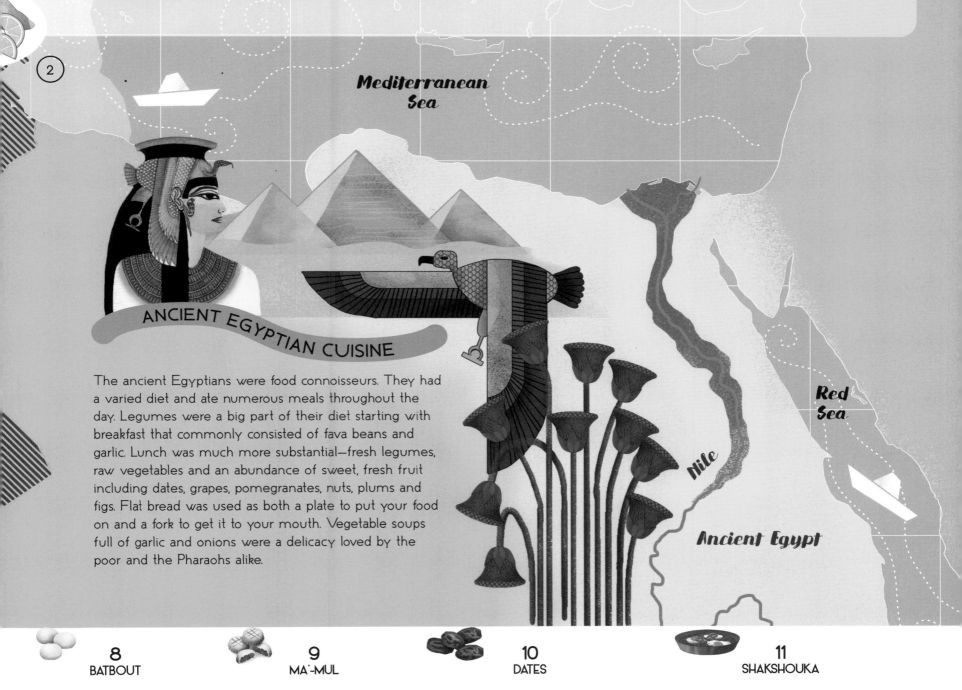

Aromas are the common thread between the various cuisines of this part of Africa that have had to adapt to the availability of ingredients in the region. The spices that color the souks, the typical noisy markets, fill the local dishes, creating harmonious condiments to eat with flat bread or couscous. The flavors of the desert deserve a special mention. The Berbers, the nomadic shepherds of the Sahara, have always raised the sheep and rams that travel with them and whose meat and milk are their main source of sustenance.

②

Mediterranean Sea

ANCIENT EGYPTIAN CUISINE

The ancient Egyptians were food connoisseurs. They had a varied diet and ate numerous meals throughout the day. Legumes were a big part of their diet starting with breakfast that commonly consisted of fava beans and garlic. Lunch was much more substantial—fresh legumes, raw vegetables and an abundance of sweet, fresh fruit including dates, grapes, pomegranates, nuts, plums and figs. Flat bread was used as both a plate to put your food on and a fork to get it to your mouth. Vegetable soups full of garlic and onions were a delicacy loved by the poor and the Pharaohs alike.

Red Sea

Nile

Ancient Egypt

8
BATBOUT

This type of bread is very simple to make: after the dough has been allowed to rise for a short time, it is cooked in a skillet on the stovetop. Its delicate flavor makes it ideal for all kinds of fillings.

9
MA'-MUL

These dry biscuits are made in tabi—finely carved wooden molds that turn each one of these cookies into a delicate, meticulous bas relief sculpture.

10
DATES

The palm trees that give us dates can live for over 300 years and produce up to 50 kg (110 lbs) of dates per year. Dates can be eaten fresh or dried and depending on their abundance in any given year, Moroccans also use them in a great variety of savory dishes cooked in the tajine.

11
SHAKSHOUKA

This simple Tunisian and Algerian dish that has also been adopted by Israeli cuisine is a pot with eggs and tomato flavored with parsley, peppers and spices served with plenty of bread for dipping.

1
ZIGNI

Served on injera, a sourdough flat bread, this spicy chicken stew is usually accompanied by vegetables and legumes and is always eaten with your hands.

2
INJERA

No need for paper plates—the edible ones used here are much better. Ethiopian injeras are thin, acidic crepes used to serve creamed soups and stews. Actually there is no need for tableware either since you can get your food to your mouth with small pieces of these crepes.

3
CASSAVA

Pasta is rarely seen on the table in Africa. Occasionally you will see cereal grains, such as rice, but tubers are the most common food, especially cassava, a root that resembles a big potato and supplies a generous dose of sugar. It is a dietary staple for many African populations. It is often reduced to flour, called tapioca and used in mashes, puddings and soups.

4
BERBERE

The Horn of Africa's own spice mix with chili pepper, ginger, cloves and coriander.

10
SELIM PEPPER

The aromatic pepper typical of this area is impossible to find in other parts of the world. Its whole seed pod is used rather than just the round peppercorns we are used to seeing. It is harvested while it is still green, but after being sun-dried for a few weeks, it assumes its usual dark color and smoky taste.

11
BAJIYA

These Somalian fritters are hot and spicy, with a green pepper and bean base. The nomadic populations used to make them using only beans, but when they became stationary, their cuisine was influenced by the coastal populations and they began to enrich their diet with other vegetables.

12
GUHWAH

Guhwah, or coffee, is made with beans roasted in a special pot heated over the coals. The coffee plant is native to these zones and in its natural habitat it can grow to be 8 meters tall!

What do PYGMIES EAT?

About half a million people in nomadic Pygmy tribes with a myriad of different languages and traditions still live in the area in and around the Congolese rain forest. They live almost exclusively on what they are able to hunt or collect in the forest (such as wild honey). They grow tubers like potatoes and cassava and they gather berries and other fruit, particularly bananas, for sustenance between one antelope hunt and another. Their diet strongly resembles that of our ancestors in the Paleolithic era. Who knows if we "supermarket goers" could survive for at least a day?

5
OKRA

Its long green pods are incredibly rich in vitamins. In Africa okra is mostly used in soups.

6
BORASH

A simple but substantial dish usually served during Ramadan, this porridge is made of oatmeal, milk, sugar and dates.

7
MATOKE

Common in Kenya, this fruit resembles a big, green, starchy banana and is used in thousands of recipes. In the most traditional recipe, these plantains are wrapped in their own leaves and slowly cooked in a particular pot, the sufuria, then mashed and served with peanuts, chicken or vegetables.

8
PEANUT SOUP

Peanuts are an integral dietary staple in Central Africa's cuisine. Their fats and nutrients make them a fundamental ingredient and this soup is genuinely delicious.

9
SHAAH

This is no ordinary cup of tea. It is a veritable essence of fragrances: cinnamon, cardamom, ginger and sugar are added to a pot of boiling hot red tea to make this relaxing drink.

CENTRAL AFRICA

In this incredibly vast part of Africa, countries and cultures are markedly different and the proof is in their cuisine. In the Horn of Africa culinary traditions resemble those of Arab cuisine, while in Sub—Saharan Africa the influence of European colonizers is evident. There is a common thread however: the one dish meal made up of a grain base covered with meat or vegetable stews. Another constant presence on the table in each of these countries is fruit: exotic, ripe, sugary and fragrant, fruit is the dessert that ends every meal here. Mangoes, avocadoes, pineapples, coconuts and bananas are an integral part of innumerable dishes, both savory and sweet.

Indian Ocean

KEDJENOU CHICKEN

Here, chickens and other barnyard animals are free to roam and eat whatever they want. They grow up lean and flavorful and if you are lucky enough to find one of them, don't let it get away! Singe the chicken to eliminate any remaining feathers then coat it in flour and brown it in hot oil till it is crispy all over. In another pan, heat some oil till it boils, then add the plantains cut into thin disks (similar to potato chips). Season with salt, lemon and chopped coriander and enjoy it while it is hot.

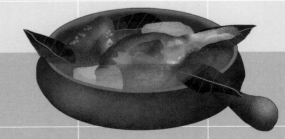

1 POTJIE

This peculiar three—legged pot is placed on the fire or on the coals to cook typical South African stews called potjiekos.

2 CORN

Corn is everywhere in South Africa! It is part of just about every meal in one form or another—fritters, omelets, polenta, corn bread, soup . . .

3 OSTRICH

Ostrich meat and ostrich eggs are common ingredients in Namibia. Bushmen make a marvelous omelet with the eggs: they break the egg and use a small stick to beat the yolk and white directly in the shell and then cook the mixture on coals in a hole in the ground.

GROWING VANILLA in Madagascar

Almost all the vanilla—this precious, expensive, aromatic bean—that enhances the flavor of our sweets and creams comes from Madagascar and part of the crop comes from the most interior part of the forest. It is the root of a wild orchid that clings to the highest trees and can be pollinated by only one kind of bee that lives here and nowhere else in the world. Once harvested, the bean is heated to 150 °F (65 °C), placed in big wooden boxes and covered for 12 hours to give it its typical brown color. Then it is dried, boxed and covered with sulfuric paper and left to develop its aroma.

Oysters and shrimp in Cape Town

4
BILTONG

They are small pieces of different kinds of meat (impala, ostrich, antelope, buffalo . . .) are dried and served as aperitifs.

5
BARBECUING

Barbecuing in South Africa is truly a ritual. Mutton, beef and lamb meat is cooked over the coals and served with a myriad of vegetables and sauces amid laughter and small talk. One of the many specialties is called skilpadjies meaning "little turtles" because of their shape. They are made of chopped liver and spices wrapped in a layer of fat before being grilled.

6
RICE

The people of Madagascar eat more rice than anyone else in the world. Every dish is accompanied by rice and consumption is estimated at about 135 kg (300 lb) per person a year!

7
MOSAKIKY

You can buy these grilled meat skewers from street vendors for a few cents. They usually come with potatoes and mango and an infinity of sauces.

8
PAP

It is a multi-purpose food: at breakfast it is served with milk, butter and sugar; at dinner with onions and tomato. The base is always the same—a mush made of white corn flour.

SOUTHERN AFRICA

The southern part of Africa, including South Africa, is a mosaic of influences and mixtures that are clearly evident in its cuisine. The conquerors who lived here brought their own influence to the typical ingredients of a land which is both fertile and rich in fish. Out of the mix came a series of dishes that are undeniably interesting in their simplicity. In addition to traditional Afrikaans recipes, dishes here have hints of Malaysian cuisine, with its abundant use of spices, and the flavors of India, whose immigrants arrived here in the 1800's to work on the sugar cane plantations. The Portuguese left their mark during the colonial period, developing a gastronomical culture that can still be appreciated in the haute cuisine restaurants of Cape Town.

OSTRICH EGG omelet

To serve 14 people, beat one ostrich egg with a pinch of salt and pepper and fry it until it is golden brown on one side. Turn it over and cook the other side. But how? Does not one egg seem like enough for all of those guests? Sure, an ostrich egg is the equivalent of 14 to 20 chicken eggs!

9
INSECTS

It is normal to eat cooked insects in this area. Catatos are caterpillars that are fried with garlic and served with rice—they taste a bit like shrimp. Gafanhotos de palmeira are toasted grasshoppers, generally eaten with funje, mashed cassava.

10
INARA

This succulent fruit is a crucial staple in the diet of the nomadic populations of this area. They use it in a number of different ways: its juice is extremely sweet, its pulp can be used to make desserts and its roots are used as a medicinal remedy. Once cooked, it can be preserved for 2 years.

11
MATATA

A strong Portuguese influence can be tasted in this dish of mussels and clams cooked in Port wine, together with chopped peanuts and fruit sprouts.

CANADA
page 66

UNITED STATES
OF AMERICA
page 68

MEXICO
page 70

CUBA
page 72

VENEZUELA
page 74

PERU
page 78

BRAZIL
page 76

CHILE
page 80

ARGENTINA
page 82

THE AMERICAS

A CUISINE FULL OF INTENSE FLAVORS AND ABUNDANT PORTIONS REFLECTS THE GENEROSITY OF THIS MIXTURE OF CULTURES.

In North America it is nearly unheard of to be hungry and not be able to find something to eat. People eat everywhere, anything and at all hours of the day. Breakfast is big—a typical English breakfast with bacon and eggs; then there is mid-morning coffee and snack and a big hamburger for lunch, which is usually enough to keep you satisfied till it is time for a muffin at afternoon snack. And then, later, a one course dinner. There is undoubtedly an enormous amount of food available and it is sometimes consumed in an unhealthy manner. As a matter of fact, many Americans, including children, are overweight and risking their health due to their excessive voracity. Putting vegetables (other than French fries) on the table at every meal and in school cafeterias has been encouraged more and more in recent years in an attempt to reverse that tendency.

First the Mayas, then the Aztecs, then the Spanish and the Africans: every population that passed through these lands left its mark on the local cuisine, adding new notes to the dishes and customs they found there. These influences gave birth to dishes that were a naturally fusion type cuisine—a kaleidoscope of colors full of joy and zest thanks to the spiciness of the chili peppers used in almost every preparation. From the land where chocolate was born (that should suffice to consider it the antechamber of heaven) this festive cuisine took off and flourished throughout the world in Mexican restaurants that recreate this vibrant, flavorful combination of food and conviviality.

1
APPLE MUFFINS

Apple muffins are a favorite snack of Canadian children. The secret to perfect muffins is to stir the dough as little as possible when you mix the wet ingredients with the dry ones—keep that in mind the next time you make them!

2
RICE PUDDING

This rice pudding is similar to porridge. Add fresh fruit and enjoy it at snack time.

3
CARAMEL PUDDING WITH HAZELNUTS AND CRANBERRIES

The great Canadian forests are the ideal place to pick berries. At the beginning of autumn, the first hazelnuts and the last cranberries—stolen from under the noses of greedy bears—end up in this delicious pudding that is popular throughout the country.

Moose

Buffalo

Pacific Ocean

Canadian bacon

The maple tree is the symbol of Canada: its leaf is on the country's flag. Its sap is used to make the world famous maple syrup, a sweetener that in cold countries like Canada is an ideal source of energy, with its vitamins and minerals. The sap is tapped in the spring and then boiled for a long time to make it into a dense, sugary syrup to pour over pancakes and doughnuts or to use in cakes.

MAPLE SYRUP

4
CANADIAN POTATOES

In Canada, like in all other cold countries, potatoes are one of the biggest crops. This tuber does not require a lot of attention to grow and it is extremely versatile in the kitchen! Potatoes are commonly served in salads with a lot of onions or as jacket potatoes they are baked in aluminum foil and stuffed with cheese and meat.

5
TROUT AND SALMON FISHING

Canada is the land of lakes, both large and small. All over the country you can find stores that rent hip boots and fishing rods to help you hook a fish to throw on the grill.

6
CHEESE AND BEER SOUP

When it is snowing outside in North America, it is time to enjoy a bowl of hot soup. In Canada one of the best is made with cheese and beer and eaten with crunchy croutons.

7
BEAVER TAIL

It is a fritter made with dough rolled out, then served with cinnamon, sugar and every other garnish you can think of: chocolate, bananas and caramel, peanut butter, and jam.

8
ICE WINE

Grapes are left on the vine until the first frost, then they are picked and used to make wine only once they are frozen. Their sugar content is very concentrated. They make a delightfully sweet wine.

Beaufort Sea

CANADA

You could never call Canada a grand gourmet country. The all-time favorite foods are still enormous sandwiches, frozen pizza and chocolate cake. Lately the country is working hard on moving towards a healthier diet; stores and stands specialized in fruit, smoothies, salads and other dishes that are still tasty but are healthier choices have begun to pop up all over.

Canadians are also very curious about foreign foods: exotic fruit and European or Asian dishes are the highlight in "fusion" restaurants where elements that come from various culture are fused together. But street food wins the popularity prize and to be eaten outside on Canada's cold streets, it has to be hot!

FRIED DOUGH

Everybody, everywhere, loves fritters—the kind you get at fairs are delicious with a sugar coating. They are easy to make: mix 250 g (2 cups) of flour, 1 tablespoon of yeast, 4 tablespoons of softened butter and enough water to make the dough pliable. After the dough rises, divide it into balls about the size of tangerines and then roll them out into discs. Fry the discs in boiling oil and when they are golden brown and bubbly, sprinkle them with sugar and eat them piping hot!

Tourtière tarts

Atlantic Ocean

9
POUTINE

This delicious dish is typical of Quebec, the French-speaking part of Canada, but nowadays you can find it all over the country. A creamy cheese and meat sauce are poured over French fries, supposedly to keep them hot. Can we pretend to believe that it is not just to make them even tastier?

10
BANNOCK

Scottish colonialists introduced this soft focaccia-like bread and it immediately became a favorite of North American natives. It was an important staple in the diets of the first explorers and fur trappers who carried it into the forests with them.

1
HOT DOG

These oblong shaped sandwiches of soft bread with a kind of sausage inside are served with mustard, ketchup and other sauces.

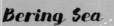

2
ITALIAN STYLE

Fettuccine Alfredo, spaghetti and meatballs... this is one of the most popular Italian—inspired dishes in America, that have absolutely nothing other than their name in common with the original Italian dishes.

Bering Sea

(9)

UNITED STATES OF AMERICA

The vastness of the United States with its countless types of agriculture and animal breeding make it difficult to put its cuisine into one category. What we can say for certain, though, is that there is a great range of variety: from the fast food restaurants present in even the most remote areas to the restaurants of the big cities. Immigrants from all over the world added their own influence and a great array of new foods to the culinary habits of the Native Americans. It is impossible to imagine a food that cannot be found in at least one of the 50 States. But there is one food that ties all American tables together: hamburgers, the only genuine national dish in the USA! They are made with any and all kinds of meat, fish, in vegetarian versions and are served with an endless variety of sauces.

Chocolate muffins

(2)

(7)

Hamburgers

PANCAKES

There is not a house in America that does not have pancakes for breakfast at least once a week, maybe with jam, maple or chocolate syrup or just sugar. They are simple and quick to prepare. Make a batter with 2 eggs, 125 g (1 cup) of flour, 200 ml (2/3 cup) of milk, 1 teaspoon of powdered yeast, 1 of sugar and 1 of melted butter. Pour the batter into a non—stick skillet by spoonfuls and when the pancakes are cooked on one side, flip them over and cook them until they are golden brown on the other.

(12) (10)

Pacific Ocean

8
DOUGHNUTS

These soft, sweet fried pastries are covered in colored frosting. Nothing gets wasted, even the little piece of dough that comes out to make the hole in the center gets fried and eaten.

9
AKUTAQ

Akutaq, or Eskimo ice cream, originated in Alaska, the land of cold and ice. To make this express version of ice cream, a mix is poured onto a frozen metal base and whisked rapidly with paddles.

10
SLOPPY JOE

A soft bun has a filling that resembles chili in this Americanized version of a recipe that originated in Central America.

11
BURGOO

"Take all the ingredients, stick them in a pan and let them cook." This is the way to make this soup according to an old American saying. Mixed meats, sauces and vegetables are shredded and served hot in sandwiches that are perfect to take to work.

3
NEW YORK CHEESECAKE

Cheese is one of the main ingredients in the batter for this cake that originated in New York City. It is aromatized with lemon and covered in caramel, chocolate or sugar coated fruit.

4
THE CORN BELT

Illinois, Minnesota, Iowa and Kansas make up the Corn Belt, the area that has raised nothing but corn since 1850. Corn is a staple in the American diet, as flour used in cakes and bread, and of course, as popcorn—a native invention!

5
SWEET POTATOES

This orange colored tuber tastes like a mix between pumpkin and potato and was well loved by the first settlers who came to this land. It can be fried or baked into a traditional sweet potato pie, a Thanksgiving classic.

6
SHRIMP AND GRITS

Shellfish and crab fishing are common livelihoods in the southern States. This dish has a semolina base covered in a tasty sauce made with shrimp—it is one of the best ways to eat them.

7
CAESAR SALAD

This celebrated salad was created by an Italian chef after World War I. Made with lettuce, chicken, croutons, bacon and parmesan cheese, and dressed with olive oil, this salad was born in Mexico, but it became famous all over the world.

What did the Native Americans that lived here eat before the arrival of the pilgrims? Their diet was based prevalently on the fruit and vegetables that grew spontaneously near their villages or in their tribal territories. They also ate game, fish, wild corn and easily cultivated beans and squash. When the pilgrims arrived in these lands, they found that these last three, sometimes called "the three sisters", were a staple in the diets of every tribe they encountered. That is one of the reasons why all three are traditionally on the table at Thanksgiving, a holiday that commemorates the story of the pilgrims that arrived in the New World, the Native Americans that helped them survive and of the friendship that developed between the two cultures.

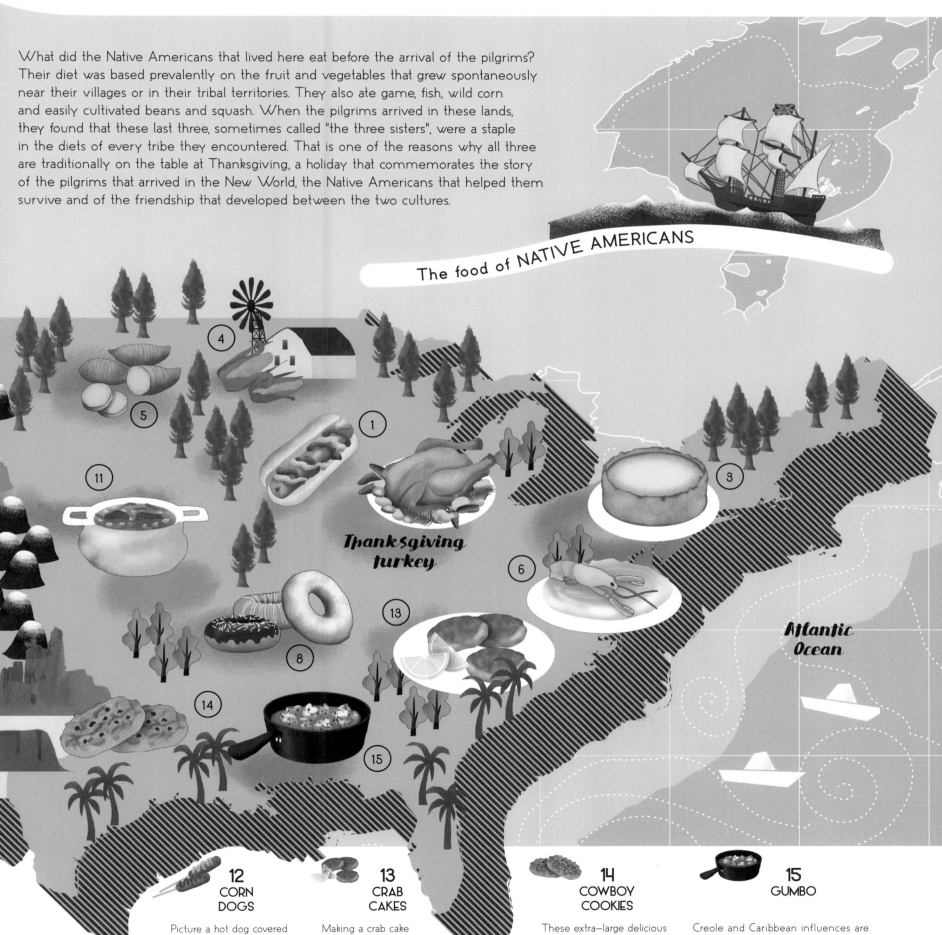

The food of NATIVE AMERICANS

Thanksgiving turkey

Atlantic Ocean

12
CORN DOGS

Picture a hot dog covered with cheese, skewered on a long stick, dipped in a batter of eggs and flour and then fried in boiling oil. Is your mouth watering yet?

13
CRAB CAKES

Making a crab cake is more difficult than it looks. Just ask the grandmothers of Maryland—they make the best ones.

14
COWBOY COOKIES

These extra-large delicious cookies are made with chocolate, oats and pecan nuts.

15
GUMBO

Creole and Caribbean influences are clearly evident in the southern regions, whose many cotton fields were worked by black African slaves in past centuries. Gumbo, an enticing soup made with chicken and shellfish, is a throwback to those times.

1
COFFEE

Since Veracruz brought the first coffee plants to Mexico at the end of the 1700s, the country has been an important producer of these precious beans. The coffee you will find here is called "cafè de olla" and is made in a terracotta coffee pot. It is usually flavored with cinnamon, chocolate and piloncillo.

2
AVOCADO AND GUACAMOLE

Avocado trees flourish in Mexico's warm climate. The green, buttery pulp of the fruit is rich in healthy fats and is used to prepare a number of dishes. To make guacamole, a popular avocado dish that has been around since the time of the Aztecs, mash an avocado with lime juice, chopped onions and tomatoes and add chili pepper.

Pacific Ocean

TORTILLAS

The dough for tortillas—Mexico's version of bread—is made with masa, a finely ground, white corn flour. The dough is divided into balls that are flattened into thin rounds with a specially made tool and cooked on a flat, red hot grill pan. Depending on the filling and the shape they are folded into, they are the base for the most common Tex–Mex dishes (burritos, tacos, tostadas . . .). If you cut them into triangles, fry them and serve them with salsa or melted cheese, they become the renowned nachos.

12
JALAPEÑO POPPERS

To make these poppers, cut open a jalapeño pepper lengthwise, stuff it with string cheese, dip it in a light batter and fry it in boiling oil.

3
FISH AND CEVICHE

The waters off of Mexico's coasts are rich with fish, which has always been a staple in the Mexican diet. One of the oldest dishes is ceviche: raw fish marinated in lemon and alcohol and flavored with spices.

4
CACTUS SPROUTS

Just like the blades of the prickly pear plant, you have to eliminate the thorns before you can enjoy this delicacy called nopales or nopalitos. They are generally boiled to get rid their slimy consistency, then eaten in salads. They taste like a cross between a green bean and asparagus.

5
TAMALES

One of the oldest dishes in Mexican cuisine, these rollups are made with corn, meat and red beans wrapped in a sheet of masa and corn husks or banana leaves and then, traditionally, steamed or boiled.

MEXICO

Mexican cuisine can be divided into two main categories. The classical Mexican cuisine, which existed before the arrival of the conquistadores; it was added to UNESCO's Human Heritage list in 2010, but it has become so contaminated by Texan cuisine that it is almost impossible to find it in today's Mexican dishes.

What you will find is Tex–Mex cuisine: unwittingly created by Mexican immigrants in the United States who could not find the ingredients to make their typical dishes and had to settle for a more Americanized version of their traditions. But there are some common elements in the two types of cuisine—the spiciness generated by using every possible kind of spices and sauces and the wealth of flavors in every dish.

6
CHAPULINES

Yes, they are grasshoppers. In some parts of the country they are served with aperitifs just as though they were potato chips.

7
PRE-HISPANIC FOOD

This cuisine, known as *comida prehispánica*, included dishes made with iguana, rattlesnakes, deer, monkeys and spiders. Ingredients that are still very well-known but not very commonly used.

FAJITAS

Fajitas are the most famous Tex–Mex dish in the world and are widely available in both meat–based and vegetarian versions to please everyone. To make them with meat, cut 200 g (7 oz) of beef or chicken into strips and marinate it in the juice of 3 limes (you can also add tequila but do not exaggerate). While the meat is marinating, slice 1 red onion and 2 red peppers and heat the grill pan. When it is red hot, cook the meat and vegetables together until they are browned. Serve the mixture with tortillas, guacamole, sour cream, cheese and fresh vegetables.

8
AQUA DE JAMAICA

This drink, also known as Karkadè, is a refreshing, thirst–quenching infusion made from red hibiscus flowers. The Portuguese and the Africans brought this custom to Mexico in the era of the conquistadores.

11
CINNAMON

Cinnamon is a hallmark of Mexican cuisine. Its slightly spicy aroma pervades both sweet and savory dishes, along with the aroma of one of the finest vanilla species that grows here.

10
AZTEC CHOCOLATE

Mexico is the land of chocolate, it originated here. It is such a treat that the Aztecs called it the food of the gods. Dissolved in boiling water with a myriad of flavorings like vanilla, chili pepper and cinnamon, ground cocoa becomes a dense, hot liquid that caresses your taste buds!

9
MOLE POBLANO

Meat, chocolate, plantains and spices come together in this hot, comforting Mexican stew that is served on tortillas. It actually comes in a thousand versions—in Oaxaca alone there are at least seven variations made with a variety of meats, fish and shellfish.

1
AJIACO

This is a national Cuban dish that can be found in various versions throughout all of South America. Bananas, corn, potatoes, beef and chicken are the base for this soup that perfectly represents all of the influences on Cuban cuisine. Spain, Africa and the Caribbean come together in this dish, named for aji, a very aromatic fake chili pepper that colors this soup with its flavor.

2
CASSAVA

In Cuba as in Africa cassava plays a fundamental role in feeding the poorest sectors of the population. This tuber is rich in carbohydrates and micronutrient trace elements. Two types of yucca grow in South America: one is sweet and can be eaten cooked or raw and the other is perfect for cooking in soups.

3
BUÑUELOS

Cubans enjoy these sweet, fragrant dumplings during the holidays. They are made with a dough of cheese and corn and can be sweet or savory.

4
MALANGA

Malanga (tannia) is another starchy tuber that has been eaten in this area since the time of the Indios. It is usually fried or boiled and is served with stews.

Atlantic Ocean

Plantains

Caribbean Sea

Most of the sugar we eat comes from this little island. Sugar cane is an enormous plant that stands out from other crops as one of the main pillars of the country's economy, but not only as sugar. From sugar cane's production waste, Cuba is able to satisfy 86% of the country's energy needs in a totally ecological way.

SUGAR CANE plantations

5
ROPA VIEJA

This is the perfect example of how nothing gets thrown away in a traditionally poor cuisine. "Old clothes" is a delicious soup made with a mix of shredded leftover meats, garlic, aji, onion and cilantro. It is usually served with fried plantains and boiled white rice.

6
MOROS Y CRISTIANOS

The allegory of this dish stems from the times of the Spanish Reconquista: the black beans are the Moors and the rice are the Spaniards. The two ingredients come together in a delicious dish that does exactly what the two populations did—create an island full of wonderful flavors.

7
CASABE

It is a bread made with grated, strained cassava that resembles a tortilla.

8
BONIATILLO

Sweet potatoes, water, eggs and sugar are combined to make this pudding. It is a filling and energizing snack.

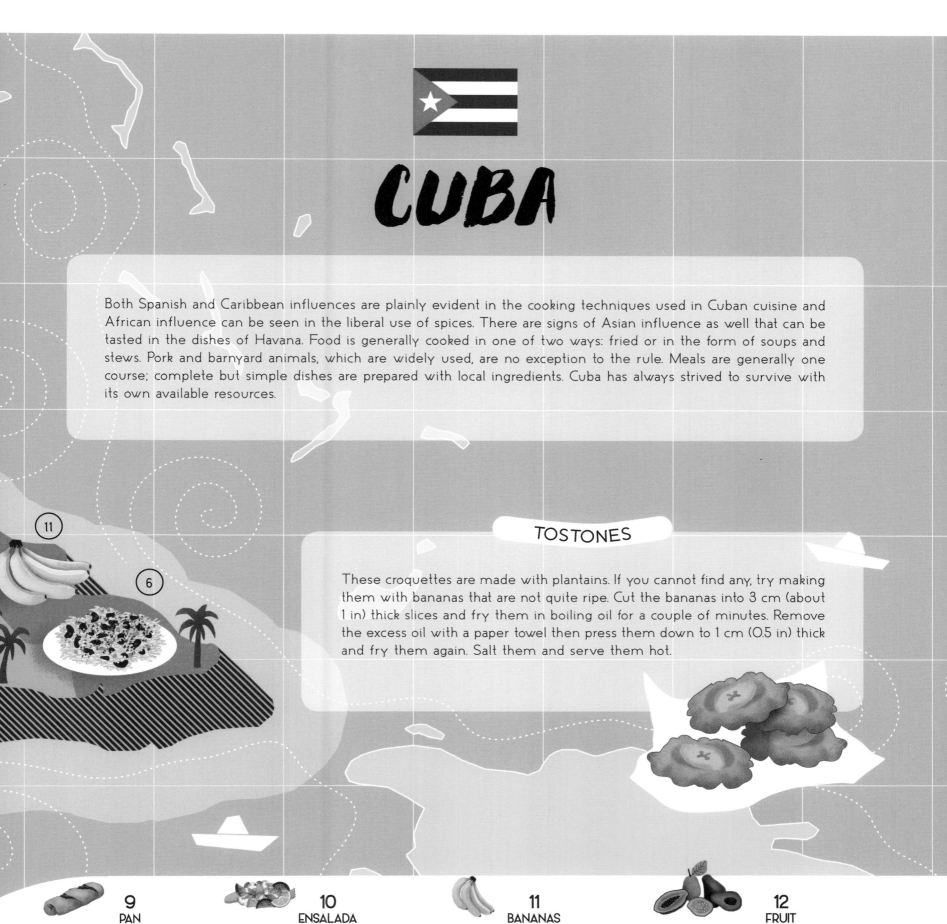

CUBA

Both Spanish and Caribbean influences are plainly evident in the cooking techniques used in Cuban cuisine and African influence can be seen in the liberal use of spices. There are signs of Asian influence as well that can be tasted in the dishes of Havana. Food is generally cooked in one of two ways: fried or in the form of soups and stews. Pork and barnyard animals, which are widely used, are no exception to the rule. Meals are generally one course; complete but simple dishes are prepared with local ingredients. Cuba has always strived to survive with its own available resources.

TOSTONES

These croquettes are made with plantains. If you cannot find any, try making them with bananas that are not quite ripe. Cut the bananas into 3 cm (about 1 in) thick slices and fry them in boiling oil for a couple of minutes. Remove the excess oil with a paper towel then press them down to 1 cm (0.5 in) thick and fry them again. Salt them and serve them hot.

9
PAN DE CHORIZO

Flavored or filled breads are often served on the island. They make for a ready-made, one-dish meal especially for the plantation laborers. One example is bread filled with hot salami and cheese and cooked in a wood burning oven.

10
ENSALADA DE AGUACATE

Aguacate (avocado) is commonly used raw in salads, often with lobster or shrimp fished from the prolific waters of the Atlantic Ocean.

11
BANANAS

The use of bananas is another indication of the influence of Creole cuisine on Cuban food. It is used in all of its many varieties in nearly every kind of dish: soups, meat dishes and rice or cut into thin slices and fried to make a tasty plate of chips.

12
FRUIT

Mango, papaya, guava (fruit with a reddish pulp and a sweet and acid aroma used primarily in juices), avocado, pineapple, lime . . . Those are only some of the kinds of fruit that you will find on the table here—sometimes as a snack, but also for dessert.

1
PABELLÓN CRIOLLO

In this typical Venezuelan dish which was born in the times of Bolivar, every ingredient symbolizes something: the black beans are the slaves, the rice represents the colonization by the Spanish, the sliced plantains are the indigenous tribes and the shredded meat is the war for freedom fought by the Latin Americans against Spanish colonialism.

2
AREPA

This Venezuelan bread is made with the flour of finely ground white corn—the most important grain in the country. It can be baked, cooked on a grill pan or fried. It may be simple or filled with stewed meat and vegetables.

3
CACHAPA

Similar to an omelet or a thick crepe, this dish is actually made with expressly ground corn, cheese and sugar, and cooked on a budare—a special stone grill plate. It is filled with cheese, folded in half and spread with butter on the outside.

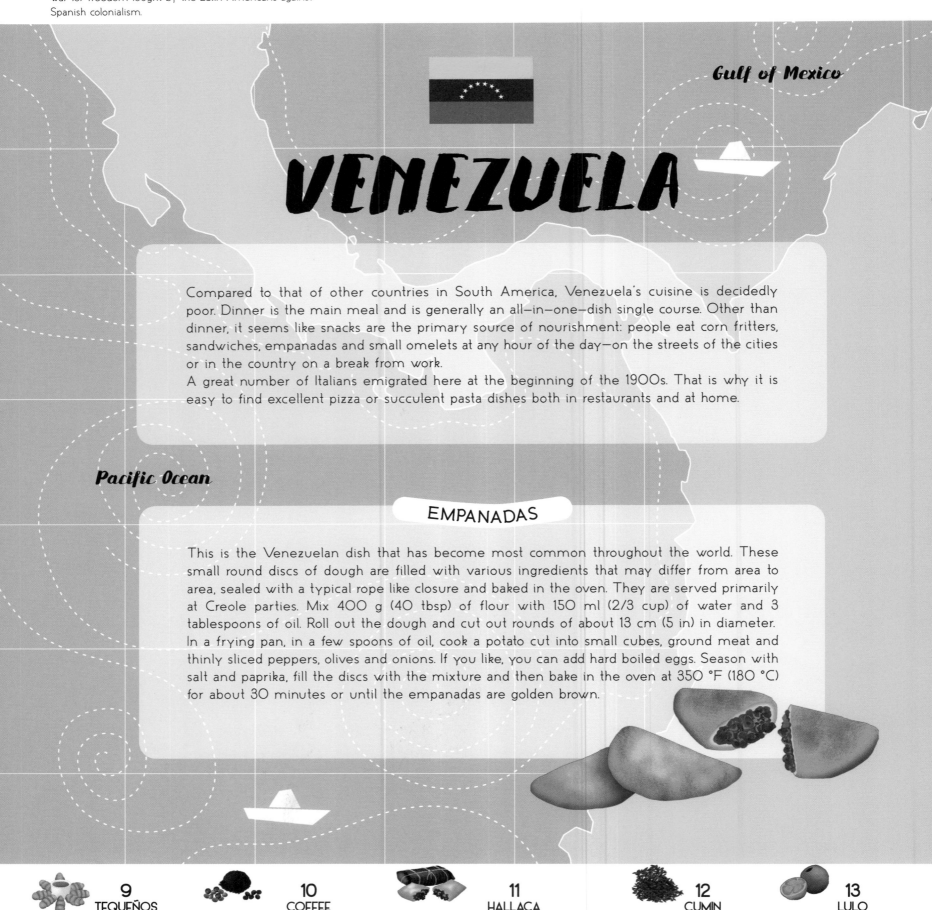

Gulf of Mexico

VENEZUELA

Pacific Ocean

Compared to that of other countries in South America, Venezuela's cuisine is decidedly poor. Dinner is the main meal and is generally an all—in—one—dish single course. Other than dinner, it seems like snacks are the primary source of nourishment: people eat corn fritters, sandwiches, empanadas and small omelets at any hour of the day—on the streets of the cities or in the country on a break from work.
A great number of Italians emigrated here at the beginning of the 1900s. That is why it is easy to find excellent pizza or succulent pasta dishes both in restaurants and at home.

EMPANADAS

This is the Venezuelan dish that has become most common throughout the world. These small round discs of dough are filled with various ingredients that may differ from area to area, sealed with a typical rope like closure and baked in the oven. They are served primarily at Creole parties. Mix 400 g (40 tbsp) of flour with 150 ml (2/3 cup) of water and 3 tablespoons of oil. Roll out the dough and cut out rounds of about 13 cm (5 in) in diameter. In a frying pan, in a few spoons of oil, cook a potato cut into small cubes, ground meat and thinly sliced peppers, olives and onions. If you like, you can add hard boiled eggs. Season with salt and paprika, fill the discs with the mixture and then bake in the oven at 350 °F (180 °C) for about 30 minutes or until the empanadas are golden brown.

9
TEQUEÑOS

These horn shaped pastries made with butter and flour are filled with cheese, and fried or baked. The result is a little cone with a gooey center that you can buy from the street vendors for an appetizer or a snack.

10
COFFEE

Venezuela is another one of the countries that cultivates and gathers these valuable beans. This precious beverage, besides caffeine, contains over 1,000 other substances, some of which have not been studied yet, that are beneficial for our health.

11
HALLACA

This dish is usually prepared in a ritual that involves the entire family at the beginning of December to kick off the Christmas season. Small cornmeal dumplings are filled with mixed meats, onions, peppers, raisins, capers and olives and wrapped in plantain leaves before they're cooked.

12
CUMIN

Cumin is the seed of an herbaceous plant. It is used as a spice in many Arab and Mediterranean cultures and arrived in South America with the Spanish and Portuguese conquerors.

13
LULO

The taste of this vegetable resembling a potato is halfway between an eggplant and a tomato. The Indios in the Andes use it for its extremely acidic juice that is full of vitamins.

4 AJÌ

This hot sauce made with chili pepper, tomato, garlic, coriander, onions and water is used as the base for many dishes.

5 CASABE

Casalbe is a thin, crunchy bread substitute. It is made with cassava and comes from the cuisine of the natives.

6 MAMONCILLO

Similar to citrus fruit, it is rich in vitamins and medicinal properties. In fact, it is still used in Venezuela's medicine as well as in its cuisine.

7 MANGO

Mango is the most widely exported fruit from this country and is also one of the most loved. Cultivating mangoes has become a source of sustenance for many.

8 TAMARILLO

Tamarillo is the fruit of the tomato tree. It actually looks and tastes a bit like a tomato, even though its fruit can be yellow or red or purple and it contains a multitude of small seeds. The plant grows wild in Venezuela and has been exported to Europe and New Zealand.

Atlantic Ocean

Corn

DULCERIA CRIOLLA

This is the name given to the traditional homemade pastries that are made with local ingredients such as papelón, corn flour and fruits like coconut, bananas or guava. These ancient sweets were prepared by the first native tribes and are still made today for banquets and holidays in homage to the products that nature provides.

14 TRES LECHES CAKE

Venezuela's most famous cake is a kind of sponge cake with condensed milk, soaked in milk and covered with whipped cream. True enjoyment for anyone with a sweet tooth.

15 CHICHA

This slightly alcoholic drink is made with fermented corn and grain mixed with fruit and cassava. It is usually homemade and is pleasantly sweet as an after dinner drink.

16 PAN DE JAMON

Bread is often baked with its flavorings already in the dough. This loaf has pieces of ham, olives, nuts and cheese. It is a typical holiday dish and like most holiday dishes, it is very rich.

1
QUINDIM

This coconut and lime–based dessert is a cross between flan and pudding. It is usually eaten as a snack.

2
CHURRASCARIAS

These small steak house restaurants serve grilled meat typical of the southern zones of Brazil and Argentina.

Coconut

The Indios that live in the rainforest have maintained a diet similar to that of pre–Columbian times. Their meals are simple and the population is made up of gatherers and hunters. Basically, their dishes are prepared using fresh water fish from the Rio (pirarucu, tucunaré, tambaqui, jaraqui . . .) with mashed cassava as a side dish. The most commonly used meats are turtle, crocodile and duck, which may seem exotic to us but are normal in these areas. The rest of their diet is made up of fruit and berries, picked and cooked in various, tasty ways.

Sugar beet plantations

6
COCOA

The nectar of the gods is produced here and in Peru. In the rainforest, you can find plantations of these big nuts with cocoa beans inside them, that when processed, dried and properly toasted become the base for the chocolate bars we all love.

What is to eat in the AMAZON RAINFOREST?

3
GUARANA

Guarana is a plant that climbs up the trees in the Amazon rainforest. Its berries are rich in an energizing substance similar to that of coffee beans and are used to make a beverage which is also called Guarana. According to a legend, the plant was created by the goddess of beauty to celebrate an extreme gesture of love. A beautiful young girl, in the hope that her lover would not be separated from her or get killed by her tribe's warriors—enemies of her lover's tribe—asked an anaconda to squeeze them in a lethal embrace. The goddess was so moved that she created this fruit whose beautiful black eyes are reminiscent of the young girl's.

4
COWPEAS

Black–eyed peas, or cowpeas, are very common in this area. Brazil grows and eats a lot of legumes—an excellent source of protein for the poorer among the population that cannot afford to eat meat. The country's main crops include just about every possible kind of bean, such as soy, and you will find at least one of them in almost every recipe.

5
CARIOCA SPICE MIX

Onions, carrots, pepper, garlic, cumin, mustard seed, rosemary and coriander are the base of this spice mix. It is commonly used to marinate meat before grilling.

BRAZIL

Brazil is a vast territory that encompasses many different climates and geological conformations. Manaus, the central region, is almost totally occupied by the Amazon rainforest. It has its own cuisine, which is quite different from that of the rest of the country where food has been greatly influenced by the Portuguese domination and its extensive use of fish, particularly salted cod.
Dried and fresh fruit, beans, cassava and vegetables are the other main ingredients in the diet of a country whose primary resources are concentrated in city centers, leaving those who live in the outlying zones to live in extreme poverty.

BEIJINHOS

These traditional sweets that are simple to prepare but genuinely delicious are a favorite at children's parties. They probably arrived in Brazil through the Portuguese convents. There are a multitude of variants: some have eggs, others are made with orange zest. They're very easy to make: put 400 g (a little less than 2 cups) of condensed milk in a small saucepan together with 60 g (1/4 cup) of butter and 100 g (1 cup) of grated coconut.
Mix well and cook until the mixture pulls away from the sides of the pan.
Leave the dough to cool, then form small walnut–sized balls. Roll them in the grated coconut and put them in the refrigerator to harden.

Atlantic Ocean

7
PAÇOCA

The people of the outlying regions, far from the city, need a dessert that gives them the energy they need to do their work. A good example is a bar made with ground peanuts mixed with cassava flour and sugar that is customarily prepared during Holy Week.

8
FEIJOADA

Feijoada, a red bean stew served with meat, boiled sausage and rice, is the symbol of Brazilian cuisine all over the world. There is no single recipe for this dish—every household has its own version passed down from its grandmothers.

9
PAMONHA

This sweet cornmeal mush is often served as a snack. Once again, corn is at the center of the country's diet—its flour is used to make cakes, cornmeal mush and simple or cheese filled bread.

10
MOQUECA

Fish, coriander, palm oil, garlic and coconut milk are used to make this typical fish soup that is been around since the 16th century in the Bahia region. The word moqueca means stew, but this could hardly be used for the meat stews we all know..

11
PALM OIL

Palm oil is the most widely used fat, much more so than olive oil. Its classic bright color turns almost every dish orange.

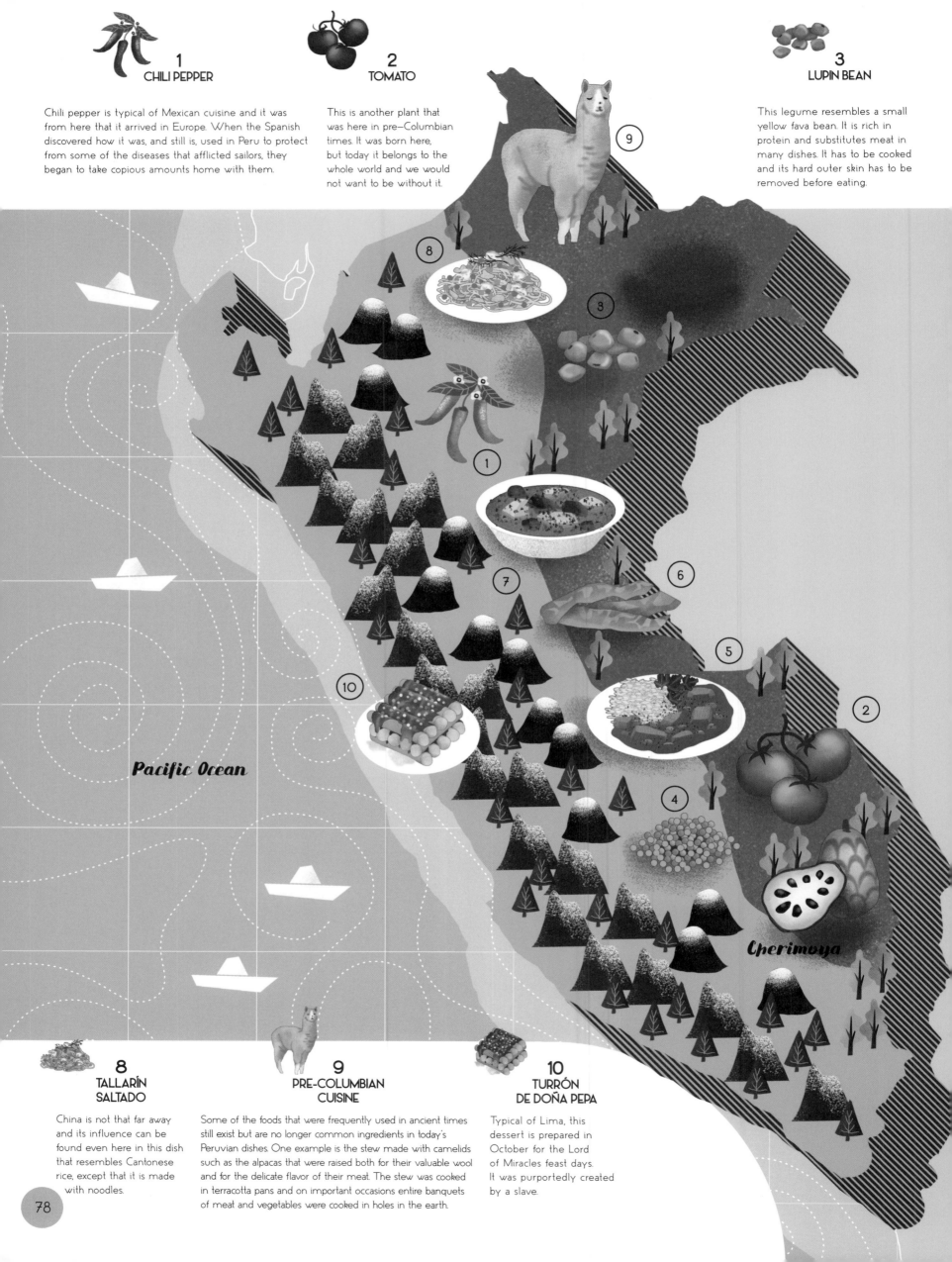

1
CHILI PEPPER

Chili pepper is typical of Mexican cuisine and it was from here that it arrived in Europe. When the Spanish discovered how it was, and still is, used in Peru to protect from some of the diseases that afflicted sailors, they began to take copious amounts home with them.

2
TOMATO

This is another plant that was here in pre-Columbian times. It was born here, but today it belongs to the whole world and we would not want to be without it.

3
LUPIN BEAN

This legume resembles a small yellow fava bean. It is rich in protein and substitutes meat in many dishes. It has to be cooked and its hard outer skin has to be removed before eating.

Pacific Ocean

Cherimoya

8
TALLARÍN SALTADO

China is not that far away and its influence can be found even here in this dish that resembles Cantonese rice, except that it is made with noodles.

9
PRE-COLUMBIAN CUISINE

Some of the foods that were frequently used in ancient times still exist but are no longer common ingredients in today's Peruvian dishes. One example is the stew made with camelids such as the alpacas that were raised both for their valuable wool and for the delicate flavor of their meat. The stew was cooked in terracotta pans and on important occasions entire banquets of meat and vegetables were cooked in holes in the earth.

10
TURRÓN DE DOÑA PEPA

Typical of Lima, this dessert is prepared in October for the Lord of Miracles feast days. It was purportedly created by a slave.

4
QUINOA

5
CARAPULCRA

6
CH'ARKI

7
CHANFAINA

This grain, whose many benefits has made it a favorite on tables all over the world, was born here. The quinoa seeds we eat in our salads come from a plant belonging to the same family as beets and spinach. It is considered a pseudo-grain like amaranth, another staple in the Peruvian diet.

Carapulcra is a sauce made with potatoes, peanuts, meat, onion, garlic and tomato that is usually served over rice and is one of the oldest dishes in the country.

A common problem in Peru has always been how to conserve all of the bounty that nature produces. Ch'arki is thinly sliced, lean meat that is put in salt and left to dry in the sun. It lasts for many months with no risk of decay.

This dish, often made with leftovers, was imported from Europe. It is made with any ingredients that happen to be available—kind of like Spanish paella. In Peru, it may even be prepared using lamb offal and beef lung.

PERU

This is the country of biodiversity. In fact, there is an infinity of plant products that exist here in the Andes and nowhere else in the world. The local cuisine reflects this fact: it is very simple, but its dishes are rich in number and variety. The more classical dishes are full of colors and flavors and offered a perfect base for the tasty inspirations that arrived from Europe in the times of Christopher Columbus. The best dishes are homemade, prepared by the able hands of the women who dedicate their time to making the soups that start off every meal and the all—in— one main course dishes served at lunch and dinner. Lima hosts some of the most renowned restaurants in the world, but it is also home to the markets where you can enjoy a snack, generally bread or potato based, made with care and displayed in orderly, tasty pyramids.

PICARONES

Made with squash and sweet potatoes, these doughnuts can be savory and eaten as an appetizer, or sweet and covered in honey. They are really simple to make. Boil 300 g (10.5 oz) of sweet potatoes and 500 g (17.6 oz) of squash cut into cubes with 2 cinnamon sticks, 1 tablespoon of anise and 4 cloves. When the vegetables are soft, drain them, take out the spices and knead them with 500 g (4 cups) of flour, 10 g (2 tsp) of yeast and 4 tablespoons of sugar. After the dough rises, make it into doughnuts and fry them in boiling oil.

POTATOES

How many kinds of potatoes do you think there are? In Peru there are 3,000 varieties, each one different from the others. These tubers have grown in the Andes for over 8,000 years and their remains can be found in pre—Columbian tombs where they were placed to accompany the defunct on his or her journey. Historians narrate that the conquistadores decided to take them back to Europe not because they tasted good, but because they were beautiful when they bloomed. Only much later did the French realize how good they tasted and how versatile they were and they began to eat them cooked. To make the potatoes last longer, they are usually dried to obtain "chuño": small potato balls that are frozen outside in the winter and then made into flour that can last for years.

1
PEBRE

As soon as you sit down at the table in Chile, you will be served hot buns with this sauce made from tomato, garlic and a lot of vinegar and chili pepper. You can enjoy them while you wait for the rest of your meal.

2
SOPAPILLA

Flour and animal fat are mixed to make these little squares of pastry that are fried in boiling oil, heavily salted and then sold in paper bags. They are one of the most common snacks in the country.

3
CHIRIMOYA

This tropical fruit is green on the outside, but with a soft, light pulp on the inside that tastes a bit like grapes. The Spanish called it "blancmange". The Chirimoya plant likes high altitudes and cold weather, so it grows well in the Andes.

4
COCHAYUYO

This seaweed grows in the gelid waters at the bottom of the ocean close to Antarctica. Once dried, it is sold in bunches, ready to be used in soups and salads.

5
SALSA DE PALTA

Avocado and yogurt are the main ingredients in this sweet and sour sauce.

CHILE

Among all of the cuisines of South America, Chilean cuisine is considered the perfect combination of the Andean flavors and those of the ocean. The arrival of Europeans during the colonial period had some influence on the country's cuisine, but Chileans managed to retain the simplicity as well as the originality of their food. In fact, on April 15th of every year, the country celebrates a day of typical Chilean food. Meals are big. They are normally made up of an entrada—the equivalent of an appetizer—followed by a main dish and some "agregados"—a series of small side dishes, not necessarily vegetables. There is always dessert on the table for special occasions!

MOTE CON HUESILLOS

Mote huesillos are peaches cooked in a sugary liquid and served cold over cooked wheat berries. Cut 4 peaches into quarters and put them in a small sauce pan with 5 tablespoons of sugar and 5 tablespoons of water. When the syrup becomes liquid and lightly colored, take it off the fire and let it cool. Then add mint leaves and enough water to reach 500 ml (2 cups). In the meantime, boil 70 g (3 oz) of wheat berries and 40 g (2 tbsp and 1 tsp) of sugar in a pan. Put a few spoons of the cooked wheat berries in the bottom of a glass, cover them with the peaches and their liquid and serve cold.

Pacific Ocean

6
LECHE ASADA

This soft, voluptuous dessert resembles pudding and is made with milk and caramel.

7
STRAWBERRIES

Strawberries are one of the most widely grown crops in Chile. They are exported throughout the entire world.

8
PANELA

Cane sugar is boiled to make this molasses which is dried in rectangular molds and cut into little blocks used to sweeten tea and coffee.

9
PARRILLADA

A dish for courageous stomachs, this mixed grill includes entrails, mammary glands and blood sausage made of pork or veal.

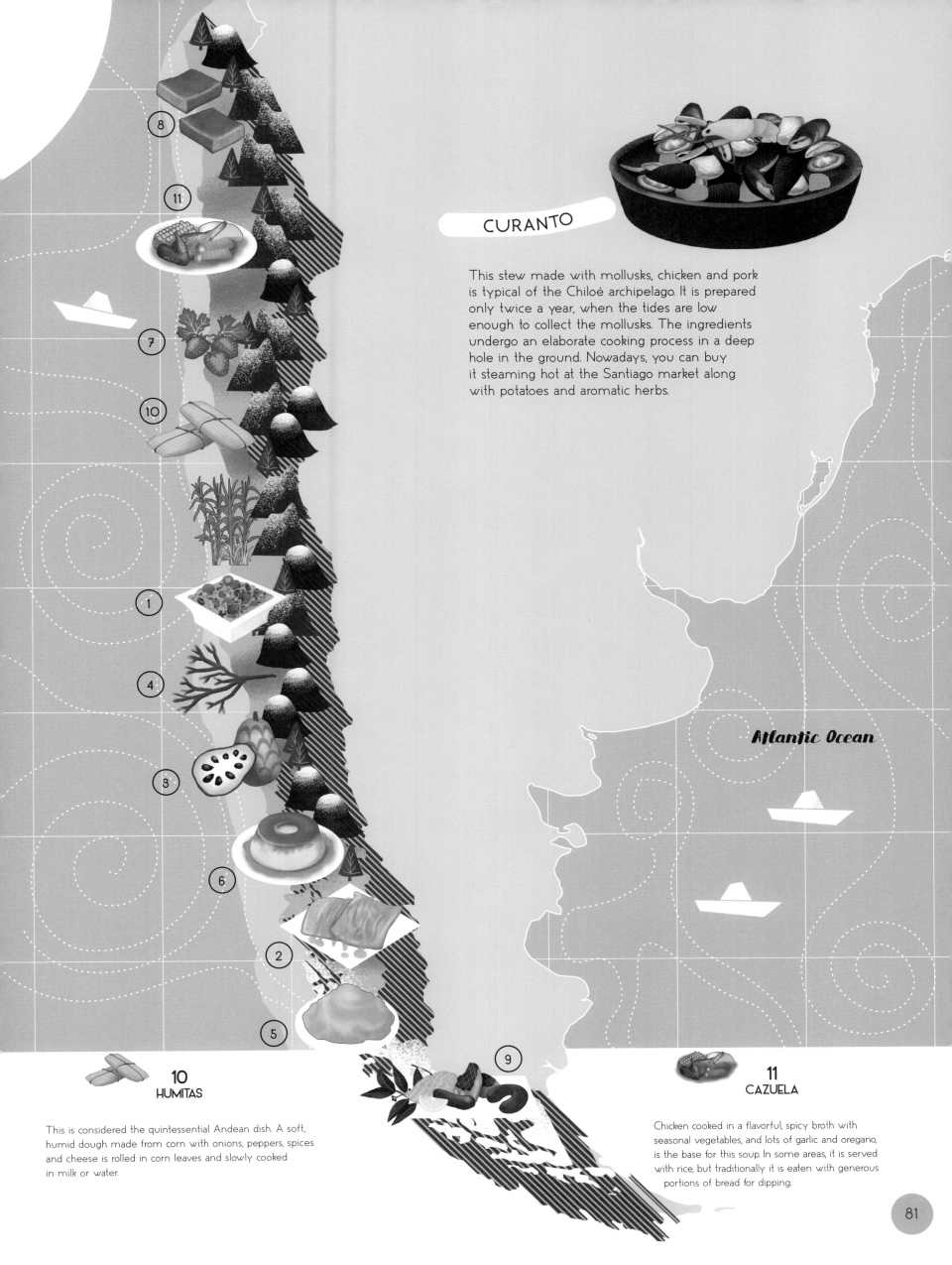

CURANTO

This stew made with mollusks, chicken and pork is typical of the Chiloé archipelago. It is prepared only twice a year, when the tides are low enough to collect the mollusks. The ingredients undergo an elaborate cooking process in a deep hole in the ground. Nowadays, you can buy it steaming hot at the Santiago market along with potatoes and aromatic herbs.

Atlantic Ocean

10
HUMITAS

This is considered the quintessential Andean dish. A soft, humid dough made from corn with onions, peppers, spices and cheese is rolled in corn leaves and slowly cooked in milk or water.

11
CAZUELA

Chicken cooked in a flavorful, spicy broth with seasonal vegetables, and lots of garlic and oregano, is the base for this soup. In some areas, it is served with rice, but traditionally it is eaten with generous portions of bread for dipping.

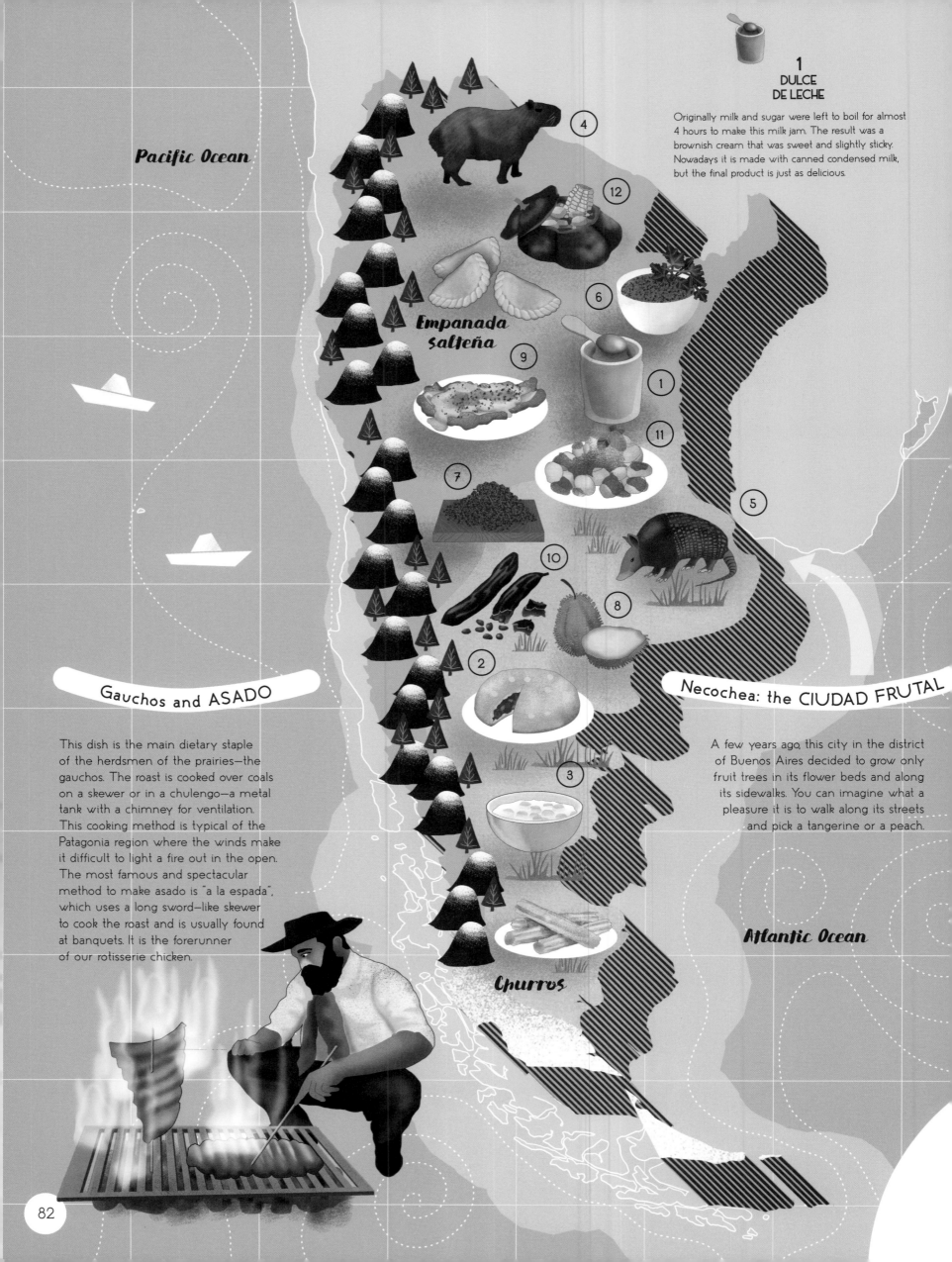

Pacific Ocean

1
DULCE DE LECHE

Originally milk and sugar were left to boil for almost 4 hours to make this milk jam. The result was a brownish cream that was sweet and slightly sticky. Nowadays it is made with canned condensed milk, but the final product is just as delicious.

Empanada salteña

Gauchos and ASADO

This dish is the main dietary staple of the herdsmen of the prairies—the gauchos. The roast is cooked over coals on a skewer or in a chulengo—a metal tank with a chimney for ventilation. This cooking method is typical of the Patagonia region where the winds make it difficult to light a fire out in the open. The most famous and spectacular method to make asado is "a la espada", which uses a long sword—like skewer to cook the roast and is usually found at banquets. It is the forerunner of our rotisserie chicken.

Necochea: the CIUDAD FRUTAL

A few years ago, this city in the district of Buenos Aires decided to grow only fruit trees in its flower beds and along its sidewalks. You can imagine what a pleasure it is to walk along its streets and pick a tangerine or a peach.

Atlantic Ocean

Churros

2
PASTEL DE CHOCLO

This sweet corn pudding can be found throughout all of South America.

3
MAZAMORRA

Typical of the poorest populations, this dish is eaten as a snack or at breakfast. Corn is boiled and sweetened with milk and sugar in a cold soup. It resembles the cornmeal mush and milk—called polenta e latte—that laborers in Northern Italy used to eat.

4
CARPINCHO

The beef from the cattle that run in the endless prairies of the Pampas is not the only kind of meat you will find on the table in Argentina. The Indios have always eaten the meat of the Carpincho, a rodent that resembles a beaver. It lives in the wild near rivers, but it is also been bred to be eaten in the last few centuries.

5
ROAST ARMADILLO

This traditional dish also comes from the Indios, but it is well loved even by those who do not live in the forest. The armadillo has a hard shell but tender meat that resembles chicken. It is generally marinated for a long time and then roasted or cooked on the grill.

6
CHIMICHURRI

This green sauce is made with a parsley base and is used to marinate meat or to serve with asado. It is said to have been invented by a certain Jimmy McCurry whose name became mangled over time.

7
YERBA MATE

This plant is used in infusion to make mate tea, a very common energizing drink with diuretic and antioxidant properties that is widely consumed by adults and children.

8
CHAYOTE

This fat, thorny squash is edible in all of its parts— leaves, fruit and roots. The fruit of the plant tastes like a mix of potato and cucumber and is generally eaten raw or in soup.

9
MILANESA A LA NAPOLITANA

This Milanese chicken cutlet with ham, cheese and tomato is an example of the extreme influence of Italian cuisine in Argentina. It is practically a cutlet pizza!

ARGENTINA

The Argentinians are an undeniably carnivorous population. The great prairies have always been home to big herds and cattle breeding is still one of the key livelihoods in the country. The multitudes of Europeans who moved here at the beginning of the 1900s seeking their fortune also brought their cuisine with them and the Italian influence in Argentina's cooking is clearly evident. Even today, many families prefer ravioli and tagliatelle to carne asada for Sunday lunch! As in all South American countries, the customs and traditions typical of the Indios that lived in this territory in the pre–Columbian era still remain intact in the cuisine of the more traditionalist populations.

ALFAJORES with dulce de leche

These double cookies with a condensed milk filling are sweet and crumbly. Knead 100 g (10 tbsp) of flour and 150 g (15 tbsp) of corn starch with 100 g (less than 1/2 cup) of butter and 75 g (5 tbsp) of sugar. Roll out the dough to 5 cm (2 in), cut out rounds and bake them in a 320 °F (160 °C) oven for 15 minutes or until they are golden brown. In the meantime place a can of condensed milk into a sauce pan, cover it with water and let it cook for an hour and a half. Open the can, spread the milk on one cookie and cover it with another. Sprinkle the cookies with abundant powdered sugar.

12
STEWS

Argentinians love meat, but not only grilled meat. Stews are common, too. An example is the puchero—a stew made with beef, pork, chicken, corn on the cob and vegetables. It is served in two courses—first the broth and vegetables and then, separately, the meat. Another common stew is the carbonada criolla made with potatoes, squash, onions, garlic, peppers and tomatoes, and seasoned with herbs. It is served with rice in a hollowed out squash.

11
ÑOQUIS Y TUCO

Tuco is a meat sauce that simmers slowly on Argentinian stoves on Sunday. It's used with egg noodles or potato gnocchi. Its Italian origin is evident; many Argentinians are sons and daughters of Italians who emigrated in search of work in the early 1900s.

10
CAROB

Carob is often called the chocolate of the poor. Its fruit is used to prepare a powder that can substitute cocoa in many desserts.

AUSTRALIA
page 86

OCEANIA

IN THE LAND OF KANGAROOS, THE CUISINE IS RICH AND EVER-CHANGING.

Oceania is the New World, a continent that was discovered only a relatively short time ago.

For thousands of years it was inhabited by Aborigine tribes with their bush food of berries and wild game, customs that have survived in some areas.

Oceania's cuisine has been heavily influenced by the domination of the English and the Irish, and by the Asian and Mediterranean immigrants that arrived after World War II.

NEW ZEALAND
page 88

AUSTRALIA

1
CHIKO ROLL

A mix of chicken meat, celery, barley, rice, carrots, onion, cauliflower, green beans and spices are rolled and heavily breaded with flour and eggs then fried. This is Frank McEnroe's version of a Chinese spring roll, easy to sell—and eat!—at football games.

Timor Sea

Kangaroo meat

Australian cuisine is a composite of the bush food of the Aborigines' and the dishes that the immigrants brought with them in the 18th century.

That is why, alongside dishes that are reminiscent of the ancestral diets of the hunters—gathers and meager dishes baked in ovens hidden in the ground, you will find typically English dishes like fish and chips, Sunday roasts and meat pies.

The traditional use of wild animals such as kangaroos, emus, zebras and crocodiles—all considered delicacies—also originated with the Aborigines.

LAMINGTONS

These little cubes of sponge cake are dipped in chocolate and then rolled in dried coconut. They were given the name of a soft teddy bear because of the "fluffy" look that the coconut gives them.

Beat 5 eggs with 140 g (9 tbsp) of sugar until they are frothy. Stir in 140 g (1 cup and 1 tbsp) of flour and 1 teaspoon of yeast. Bake the batter in a 350 °F (180 °C) oven for 40 minutes. When the cake is cooled, cut it into cubes. While the cake is cooling, sift 300 g (almost 2 cups) of powdered sugar together with 40 g (7 tbsp) of cocoa powder and stir it into 35 g (2 tbsp) of melted butter. Dip each cake cube into the glaze and then roll it in grated coconut. Let it dry and enjoy!

For years, Australians were indifferent to what was put on the table. But as they began to think about their health, this country became the homeland of organic food and what is known as superfood—berries and fruits rich in nutrients, true natural supplements that the local flora readily offers. The range of organic products available in supermarkets is growing and becoming more affordable and the country's diet is getting healthier and more balanced.

ORGANIC food

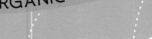

12
ANZAC COOKIES

These cookies are made in memory of the soldiers that fell during the First World War in the same way their wives used to make them—with coconut, oats and maple syrup. They did not cost much to make, they lasted a long time and they were adapt for the trenches.

11
MEAT PIE

If you happen to be in Australia and are feeling hungry after dinner, get your energy back with one of these meat pies. You can get them with ground meat, sauce, mushrooms and vegetables—or in a vegetarian version if you prefer.

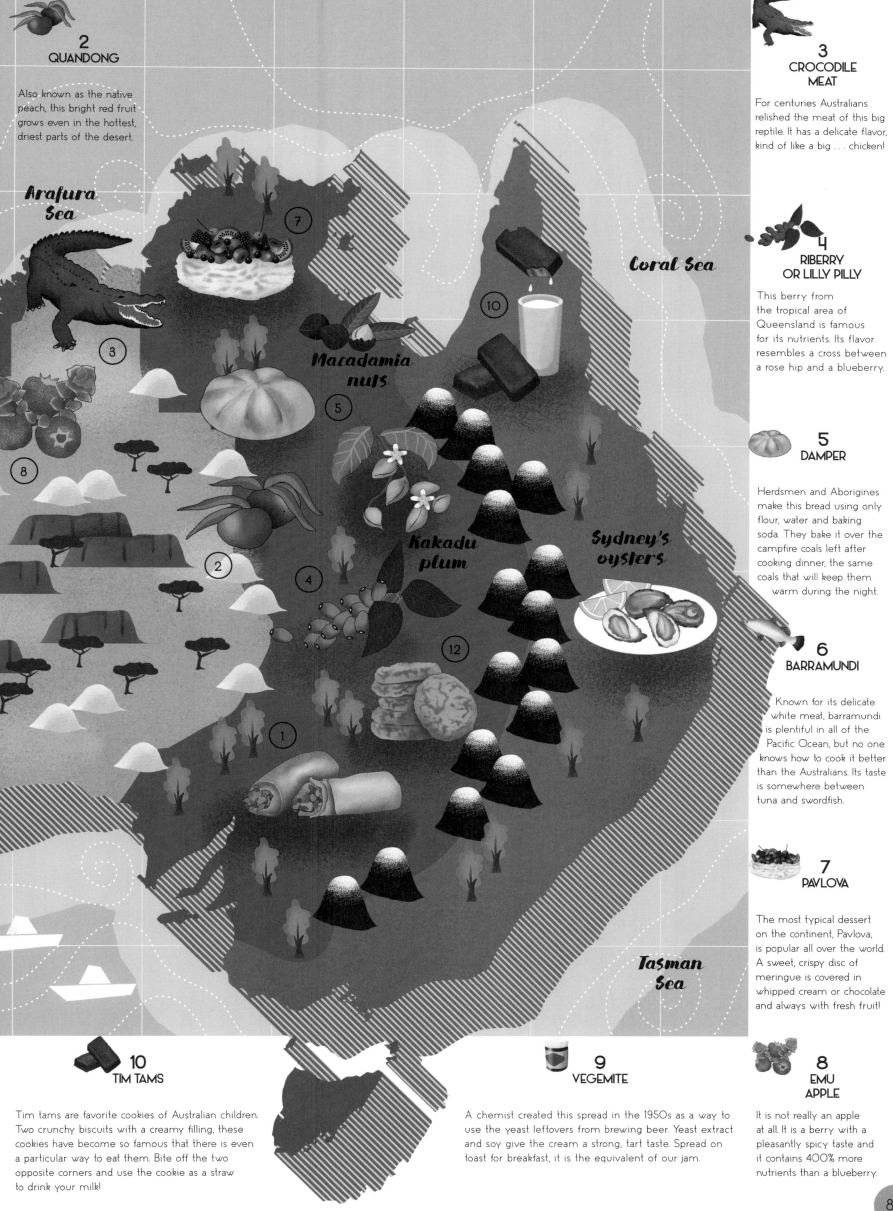

2
QUANDONG

Also known as the native peach, this bright red fruit grows even in the hottest, driest parts of the desert.

Arafura Sea

3
CROCODILE MEAT

For centuries Australians relished the meat of this big reptile. It has a delicate flavor, kind of like a big . . . chicken!

4
RIBERRY OR LILLY PILLY

This berry from the tropical area of Queensland is famous for its nutrients. Its flavor resembles a cross between a rose hip and a blueberry.

Coral Sea

Macadamia nuts

5
DAMPER

Herdsmen and Aborigines make this bread using only flour, water and baking soda. They bake it over the campfire coals left after cooking dinner, the same coals that will keep them warm during the night.

Kakadu plum

Sydney's oysters

6
BARRAMUNDI

Known for its delicate white meat, barramundi is plentiful in all of the Pacific Ocean, but no one knows how to cook it better than the Australians. Its taste is somewhere between tuna and swordfish.

7
PAVLOVA

The most typical dessert on the continent, Pavlova, is popular all over the world. A sweet, crispy disc of meringue is covered in whipped cream or chocolate and always with fresh fruit!

Tasman Sea

10
TIM TAMS

Tim tams are favorite cookies of Australian children. Two crunchy biscuits with a creamy filling, these cookies have become so famous that there is even a particular way to eat them. Bite off the two opposite corners and use the cookie as a straw to drink your milk!

9
VEGEMITE

A chemist created this spread in the 1950s as a way to use the yeast leftovers from brewing beer. Yeast extract and soy give the cream a strong, tart taste. Spread on toast for breakfast, it is the equivalent of our jam.

8
EMU APPLE

It is not really an apple at all. It is a berry with a pleasantly spicy taste and it contains 400% more nutrients than a blueberry.

1
CHOCOLATE BUTTER

One of the country's largest producers of cheese got together with a leading chocolatier to create this delicious spread—perfect on bread for breakfast.

2
GREEN MUSSELS

Uncontaminated ocean waters offer a multitude of delicious fish and shellfish. One that is gaining in popularity is the green mussel. It owes its color to a particular seaweed that the Maoris believe has great medicinal properties.

3
TOHEROA AND TUATUA

These two crustaceans are common only in this particular part of the ocean. Raw or in simple preparations that exalt their saltwater flavor, they are a favorite with tourists.

4
HOKEY POKEY BISCUITS

It is a particularly original cookie; baking soda is added to a base made with caramel, heavy cream and honey to make a light batter that becomes hard and airy and melts in your mouth when it is baked and cooled. Perfect to serve with a bowl of ice cream.

5
KUMARA

The Maoris use this creamy, delicate sweet potato in a number of dishes including rēwena parāoa, a sourdough bread. The grated potato is left to ferment and then used as a substitute for yeast.

NEW ZEALAND

Though the national cuisine is particularly refined in New Zealand's cities, it is surprisingly simple in the outlying areas. New Zealanders raise and eat a lot of meat, especially sheep and goat. Dairy is one of the country's most thriving industries, so ice cream, cheese and milk are a constant on New Zealand tables. Fish and mollusks are also readily available and have been around since ancient times, even in the rather primitive cuisine handed down by the Maori.

An interesting fact about restaurants: there are two types—those that have a license to sell alcohol and those that do not. When dining in those that do not, BYOB, or Bring Your Own Bottle, is the way to go.

AFGHANS BISCUITS

Chocolate, lots of chocolate, and cornflakes come together in these easy to make cookies. Blend 40 g (1/2 cup) of cornflakes with 200 g (a little less than 1 cup) of softened butter, 180 g (1 cup and 1/2) of flour, 2 tablespoons of cocoa powder, 5 walnuts and 100 g (1/2 cup) of sugar. Divide the dough into small balls and bake them in a 350 °F (180 °C) oven for 15 minutes. Let them cool. In the meantime, melt 100 g (1/2 cup) of chocolate, add 100 g (1/2 cup) of heavy cream and let it cool. Dip one end of each cookie into the chocolate, put a walnut in the center and let it cool.

Tasman Sea

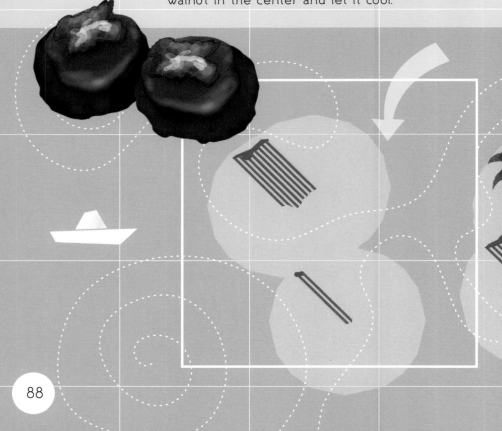

8
MEAT PIE

New Zealanders are definitely carnivorous and they love their meat pies. They can be cooked in a variety of sauces. They usually are covered in mashed potato or puff pastry crust and then baked in the oven.

6 FEIJOA

This sweet, intensely fragrant fruit tastes like a combination of pineapple and kiwi and has the consistency of a strawberry.

7 PĀUA

This mollusk is also known as "ocean ear" here probably because of the shape of the single shell that protects it like a canopy. The best ones come from Bluff Island. Pāua fritters are a popular dish.

HĀNGI

New Zealand cuisine has not got a particularly long history but the Maori's cooking techniques, used long before the time of the conquerors, certainly do. Hāngi is one of the oldest of these techniques. A hole is excavated in the ground. Food is placed in a basket and lowered onto fiery hot rocks and covered with earth and a wooden board to cook slowly. This method is still used on special occasions, particularly to cook mutton with vegetables.

Kiwi

Pacific Ocean

9 CABBAGE TREE

No one knows where it got its name. It is a very tall tree, native to Oceania and has been around for thousands of years. The Maoris use it in any number of ways: the sugar-rich leaves are added to meat dishes to make them sweet but they are also used to make a beer-like beverage.

10 HUHU GRUBS

These white cockroach larvae are typical of the Maoris' traditional diet and can be found only in New Zealand. Their high fat content makes them a great source of energy. They can be up to 60 mm (2.5 in) long. To eat one, hold it by the head and bite into the body. Eaten raw they taste a bit like peanut butter but cooked, their flavor changes. The skin tastes a bit like fried chicken and the inside tastes something like almonds.

11 KIWI

The kiwi is the country's quintessential fruit. They even make wine with it. The mild climate favors a plentiful harvest every year. Did you know that there is also a bird with the same name that is round and brown just like the fruit? It cannot fly but it was named National Bird of New Zealand anyway!

BREAKFAST AROUND THE WORLD

We all know that breakfast is the most important meal.
But do we know how children around the world start their day? You might be surprised!

KENYA

A piece of fruit, usually a banana, uji, which is porridge made with millet, amaranth or sorghum flour and unleavened bread.

SWEDEN

Cucumbers, tomatoes, toast, hard boiled eggs and herring.

JAPAN

Miso soup, pickled vegetables and white rice.

UNITED KINGDOM

Grilled tomatoes, scrambled eggs, bacon and sausage.

VIETNAM

Tea and phở, a rice noodle soup with beef and chicken.

BRAZIL

Toast and fresh papaya.

CUBA

Tostadas and coffee with milk.

INDIA

Dosa, a thin pancake, chutney, a sweet and sour vegetable jam, and sambar, a stew with vegetables and legumes.

BAHAMAS

Corn porridge and shrimp stew.

AUSTRALIA

Corn flakes and milk with vegemite on toast.

EGYPT

Ful medames,
a stew made
with tick beans
and chickpeas,
and bread.

ICELAND

Runny porridge with
raisins and walnuts.

SOUTH AFRICA

Putu pap,
a multigrain
porridge
with stew.

MEXICO

Eggs with
hot sauce and
corn tortillas.

ITALY

Cappuccino,
cookies, bread
and jam.

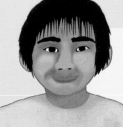

FRANCE

Coffee with milk
and croissant.

ETHIOPIA

Genfo, a stiff
porridge with a
hole in the middle
for yogurt and
spices.

BOLIVIA

Salteñas, tasty
pies with meat
or with vegetables
and cheese.

UNITED STATES OF AMERICA

Pancakes with
jam, fruit juice
and crispy bacon.

MOROCCO

Olive oil bread with
sugar and mint tea.

TURKEY

Sucuk, dried sausage
with cucumbers
and tomatoes.

HOLIDAYS AROUND THE WORLD

A holiday would not be a holiday without the special dishes that traditionally go with it. All over the world, eating is an important part of celebrating festivities regardless of nationality or religion. And not every celebration has to be in honor of the holidays on your calendar. Why not create one of your own? Invite your friends from different corners of the world and sample some of their traditional dishes.

IN SWEDEN ...

a large salt-cured ham is left to brine for a couple of days then baked with molasses and mustard to serve as the main dish on Christmas day.

IN THE UNITED STATES ...

Christmas pudding is a rich bread pudding served with butter cream and, just for the adults, a bit of whiskey cream too.

IN ITALY ...

panettone is one of the traditional Christmas cakes, a soft sweet bread loaf with candied fruit and raisins that is as fluffy as a pillow. At Christmas in Italy, choosing between panettone and pandoro is always a dilemma.

IN GERMANY ...

stollen, a delicious, fragrant cake, is a cylinder of marzipan wrapped in leavened dough symbolizing the birth of Jesus.

IN SOUTH AMERICA ...

on Christmas days, hojuelas, corn fritters fried in hot oil, are served with hot cream, chocolate and guava paste.

THE ANGLO-SAXONS ...

usually prepare an Easter breakfast on Holy Friday. They bake hot-cross buns, little sweet rolls with raisins and cinnamon that have a glaze cross on top.

IN BULGARIA . . .

kozunak is the sweet, crown-shaped bread with nuts that you can bake while you are coloring the eggs for your Easter egg hunt.

IN MIDDLE EAST . . .

matzah brei is a small omelet traditionally made with eggs and matzo at Passover, the Jewish Easter.

IN INDIA . . .

Diwali, the Hindu Festival of Lights, would not be complete without mithai, traditional little sweets made with flour, jaggery and honey with a variety of fillings and fried in ghee.

FOR THE BUDDHISTS . . .

Vesak celebrates the life of Buddha, harmony and supreme peace. On this occasion, the food is not as important as the act of sharing the meal among the monks and the laymen who sit together around the table for the celebration.

IN CHINA . . .

little flower rolls are always on the table for the Chinese New Year. They are usually shaped like flowers or animals and the head of the family gets one with a piece of fruit inside as a sign of prosperity for the coming year.

IN NORTHERN AFRICA . . .

Iftar is the evening meal during Ramadan, the month of fasting. It is the only meal you are allowed to eat in a 24-hour period so it has to be substantial with energizing ingredients. Dates, dried fruit, and delectable sugar doughnuts whit lemon and rose water—called jalebi—are favorites.

IN POLAND . . .

Hanukkah is the Jewish Festival of Lights celebrated a few days before Christmas, around the time of the winter solstice. Babka is a sweet, soft yeast cake with chocolate or almonds and walnuts that absolutely must be on the table to celebrate this occasion.

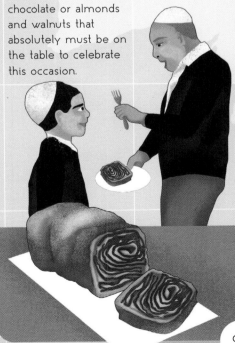

93

Do you feel like tasting something?

Well then, run to the kitchen, open the pantry
and find all of the ingredients!

The only thing you have to do now is decide which country
you would like to have dinner in and then prepare
the recipe we chose for you.

Throw open your doors and invite your friends.

Your neighbors and acquaintances from countries both
near and far: each of them, just like you, has a wealth
of traditions and habits just waiting for you to discover!

Why not organize a party,

and fill the table with the foods you love, all prepared by you?

So you see?
A trip around the world
without ever leaving your kitchen!

Genny Gallo

Genny Gallo was born in Italy.
She considers herself a child of the
1980s through and through. She has
loved food since she was a little girl
and used to closely observe her
grandmother cook while she listened
to South American soap operas
in the background. As she grew up,
her appreciation for good food
endured and her curiosity and
passion brought her to write about
ingredients and stories for her blog,
alcibocommestibile.com, as well
as in books and magazines,
both online and in print.

Annalisa Beghelli

Annalisa Beghelli earned her degree
in architecture at the University
of Venice in 2006, but after working
for four years she chose to follow
her passion for drawing and make it
her new career. In 2011, she earned
a specialty degree in illustration
and editorial planning from the
international masterclass MiMaster
in Milan, which is where she currently
lives. She is a freelance illustrator
and in 2017, she founded FAI 31,
a company that develops innovative
communication and training projects
based on the use of innovative
editorial instruments.

Graphic Design
Annalisa Beghelli

WS KIDS
WHITE STAR KIDS

White Star Kids® is a registered trademark property of White Star s.r.l.

© 2018 White Star s.r.l.
Piazzale Luigi Cadorna, 6
20123 Milan, Italy
www.whitestar.it

Translation: Iceigeo, Milan (Cynthia Koeppe, Katherine M. Clifton, Simone Gramegna, Lorenzo Sagripanti)

ISBN 978–88–544–1279–8
1 2 3 4 5 6   22 21 20 19 18

Printed in Italy by Rotolito S.p.A. – Seggiano di Pioltello (MI)